BALONEY
AND FRIENDS

BALONEY

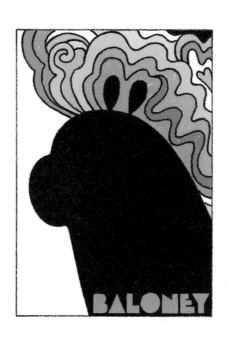

FOR ZACH, LYDIA, OSKAR, AND TEDDY

ABOUT THIS BOOK

This book was edited by Andrea Spooner and art directed by Dave Caplan. The production was supervised by Lillian Sun, and the production editor was Lindsay Walter-Greaney. The text was hand-lettered by Greg Pizzoli.

Little, Brown and Company • Hachette Book Group • 1290 Avenue of the Americas, New York, NY 10104 • Visit us at LBYR.com • First Edition: February 2022 • Little, Brown and Company is a division of Hachette Book Group, Inc. • The Little, Brown name and logo are trademarks of Hachette Book Group, Inc. • The publisher is not responsible for websites (or their content) that are not owned by the publisher. • Library of Congress Cataloging-in-Publication Data • Names: Pizzoli, Greg, author. • Title: Baloney and friends: dream big! / Greg Pizzoli. • Other titles: Dream big! • Description: First edition. | New York ; Boston: Little, Brown and Company, 2022. | Series: Baloney & friends | Summary: "Baloney and friends continue their adventures, which include a birthday cake mishap, a tricky bargain, a painting surprise, and the discovery that the best moments are shared with friends"—Provided by publisher. • Identifiers: LCCN 2021027524 | ISBN 9780316218559 (paper over board) | ISBN 9780316216395 (ebook) | ISBN 9780316369718 (ebook) | ISBN 9780316369817 (ebook) • Subjects: CYAC: Graphic novels. | Animals—Fiction. | Friendship—Fiction. | LCGFT: Graphic novels. • Classification: LCC PZ7.7.P54 Bah 2022 | DDC 741.5/973—dc23 • LC record available at https://lccn.loc.gov/2021027524 • ISBNs: 978-0-316-21855-9 (paper over board), 978-0-316-21639-5 (ebook), 978-0-316-36971-8 (ebook), 978-0-316-36981-7 (ebook) • Printed in CHINA • APS •

10 9 8 7 6 5 4 3 2 1

ONEY AND FRIENDS
DREAM BIG!

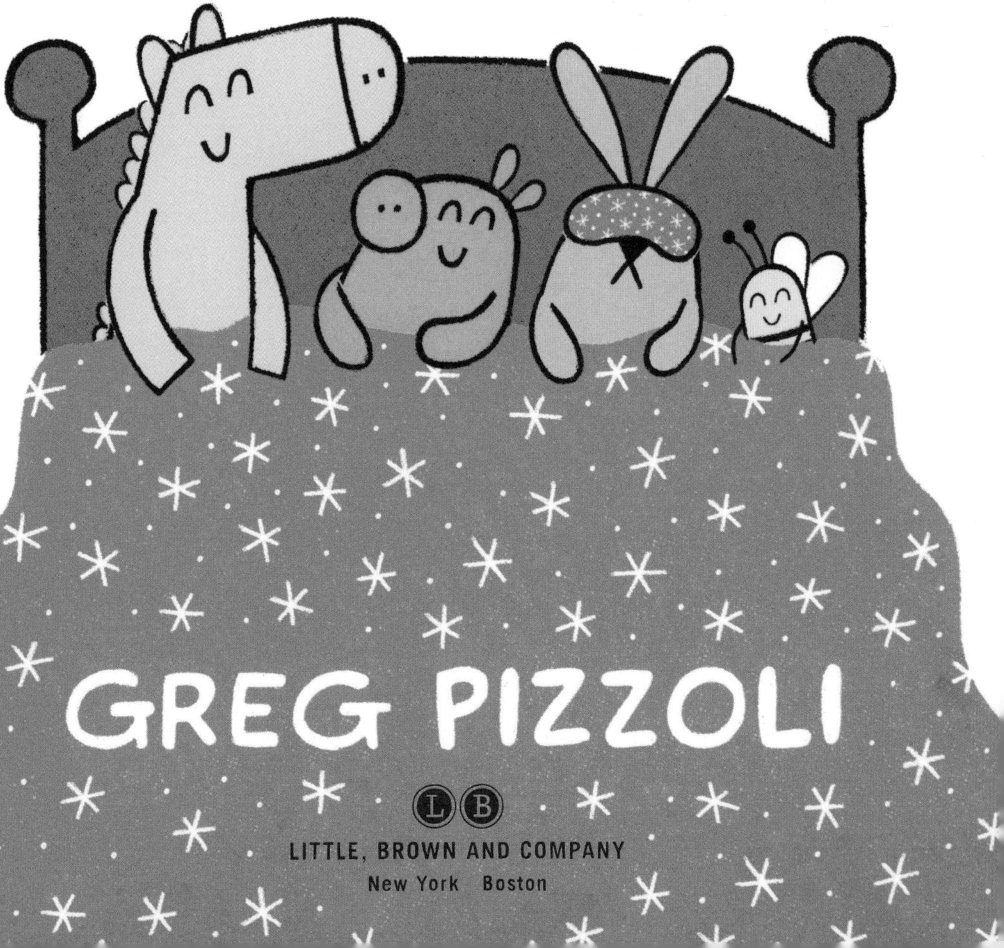

GREG PIZZOLI

LB
LITTLE, BROWN AND COMPANY
New York Boston

TABLE OF CONTENTS

FIRST UP... BALONEY + FRIENDS SELL OUT! AN INTRODUCTION OF SORTS PAGE 2

THIS FIRST BIG STORY IS A PIECE OF CAKE IT STARTS ON PAGE 12

MINI-COMIC BAD DREAM THAT'S ON PAGE THIRTY-TWO

AND THEN! PEANUT D. HORSE STARS IN SPARE CHANGE STARTING ON PAGE 34

MINI-COMIC GOOD SPORTS THAT'S ON PAGE FIFTY-EIGHT

DON'T MISS THIS! ON PAGE 60 THE PAINTING

THEN, MY FRIENDS, ON PAGE 80 I'M AFRAID WE HAVE REACHED... THE END

BONUS! PAGE 82 HOW TO MAKE A MINI-BOOK! USING ONE SHEET OF PAPER!

HOORAY.

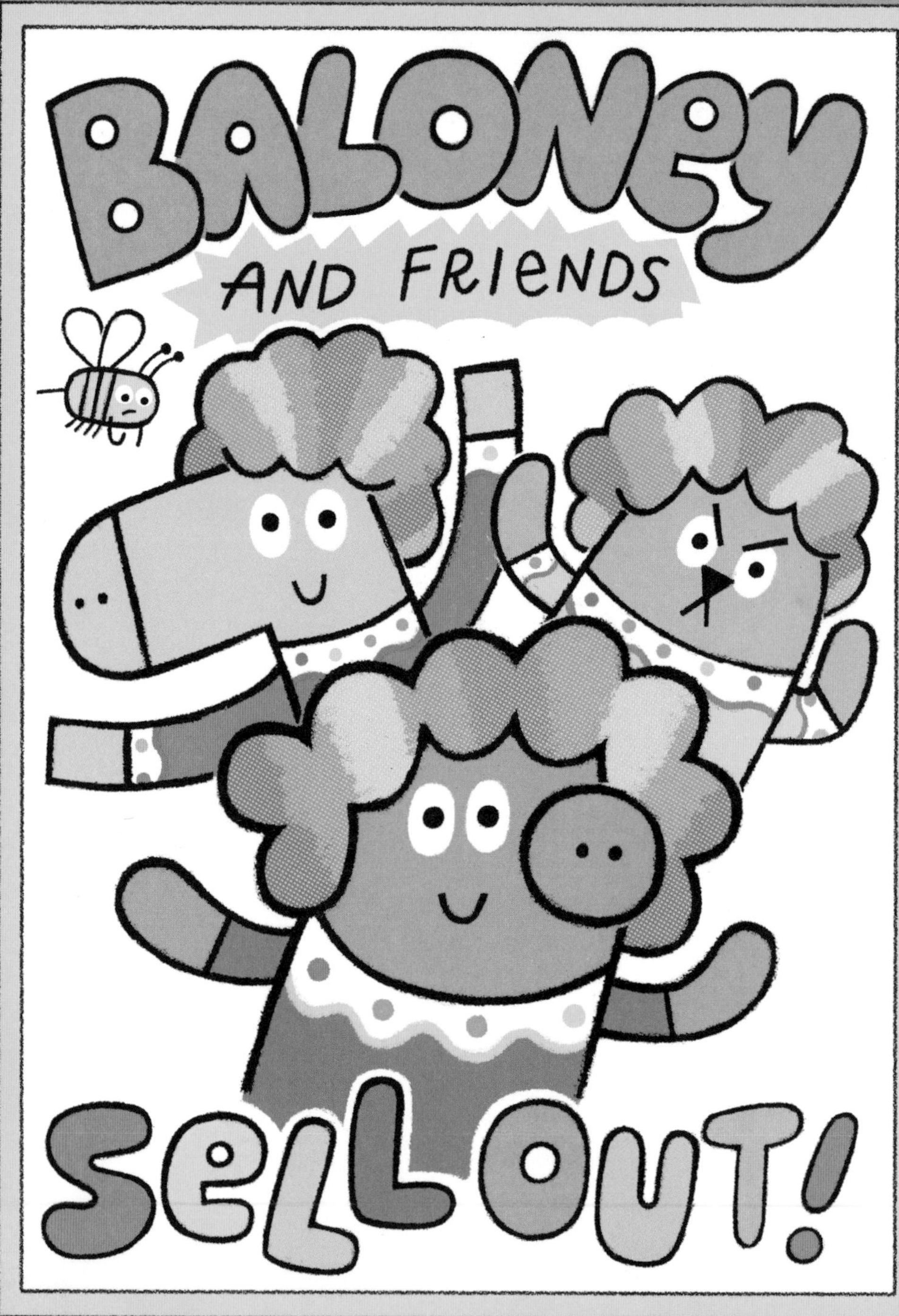
BALONEY
AND FRIENDS
SELL OUT!

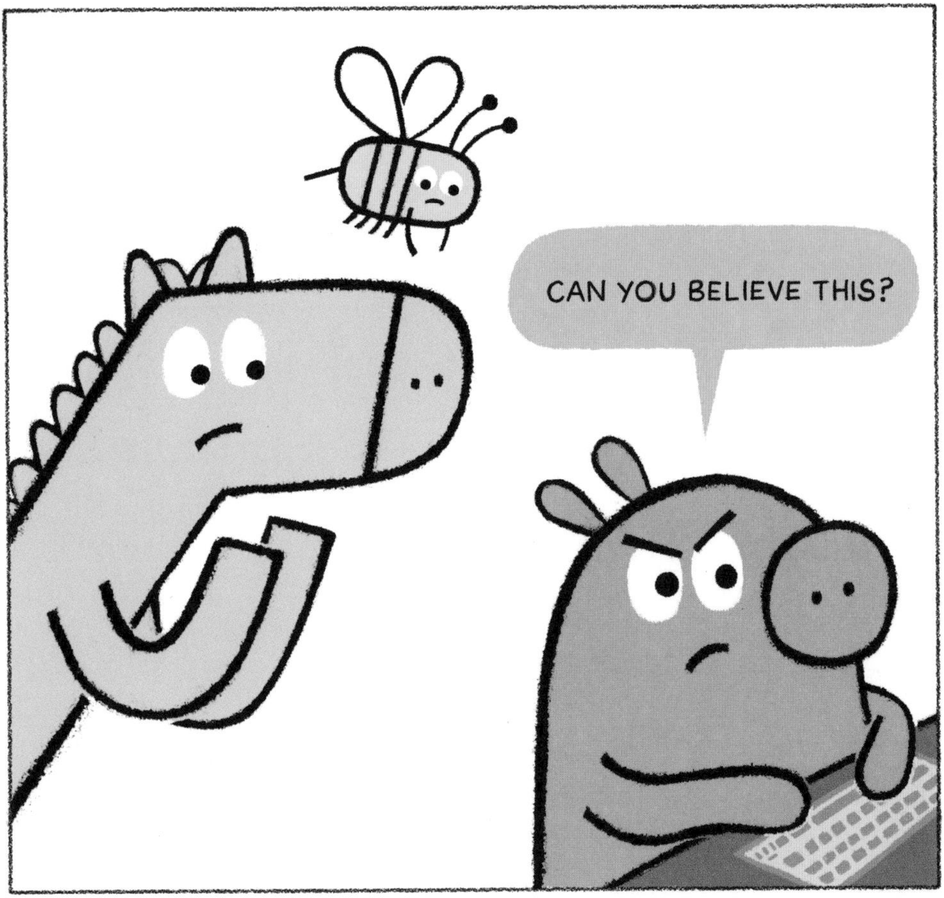
CAN YOU BELIEVE THIS?

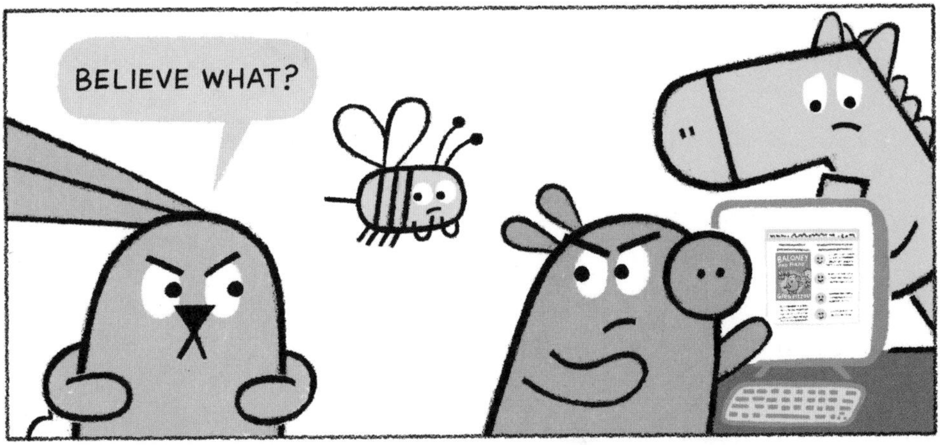
BELIEVE WHAT?

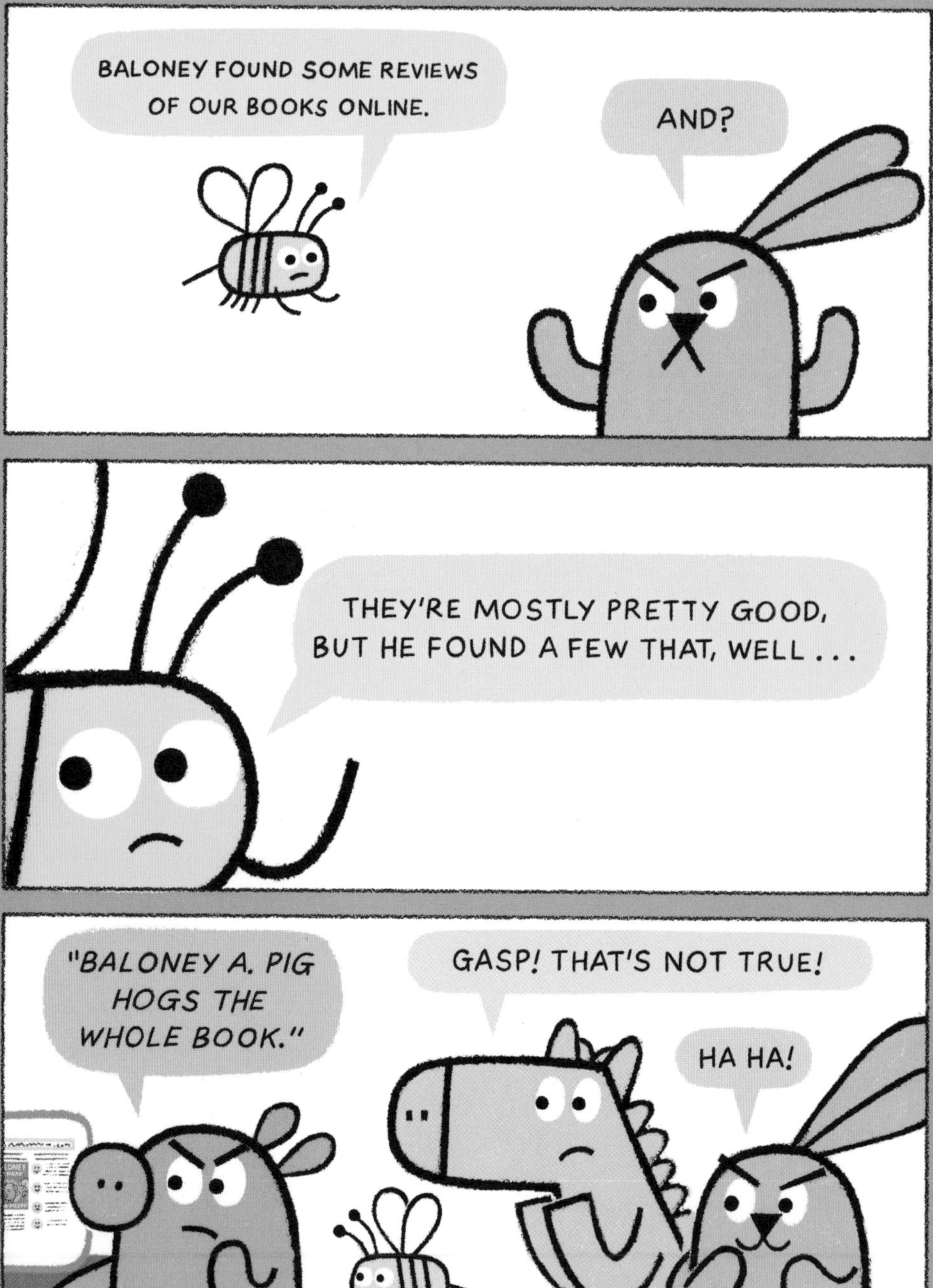
BALONEY FOUND SOME REVIEWS OF OUR BOOKS ONLINE.
AND?
THEY'RE MOSTLY PRETTY GOOD, BUT HE FOUND A FEW THAT, WELL . . .
"BALONEY A. PIG HOGS THE WHOLE BOOK."
GASP! THAT'S NOT TRUE!
HA HA!

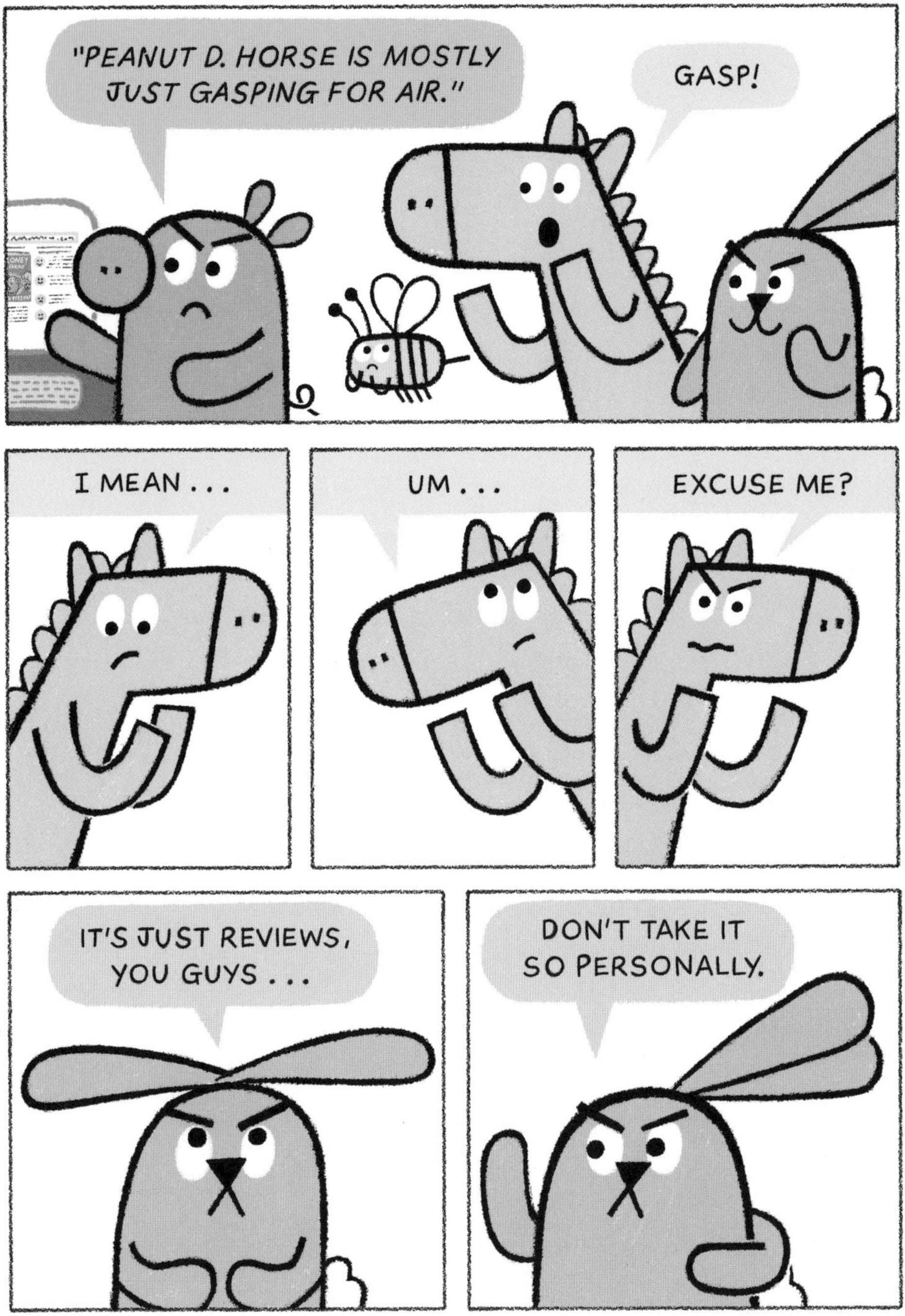

"PEANUT D. HORSE IS MOSTLY JUST GASPING FOR AIR."
GASP!
I MEAN . . .
UM . . .
EXCUSE ME?
IT'S JUST REVIEWS, YOU GUYS . . .
DON'T TAKE IT SO PERSONALLY.

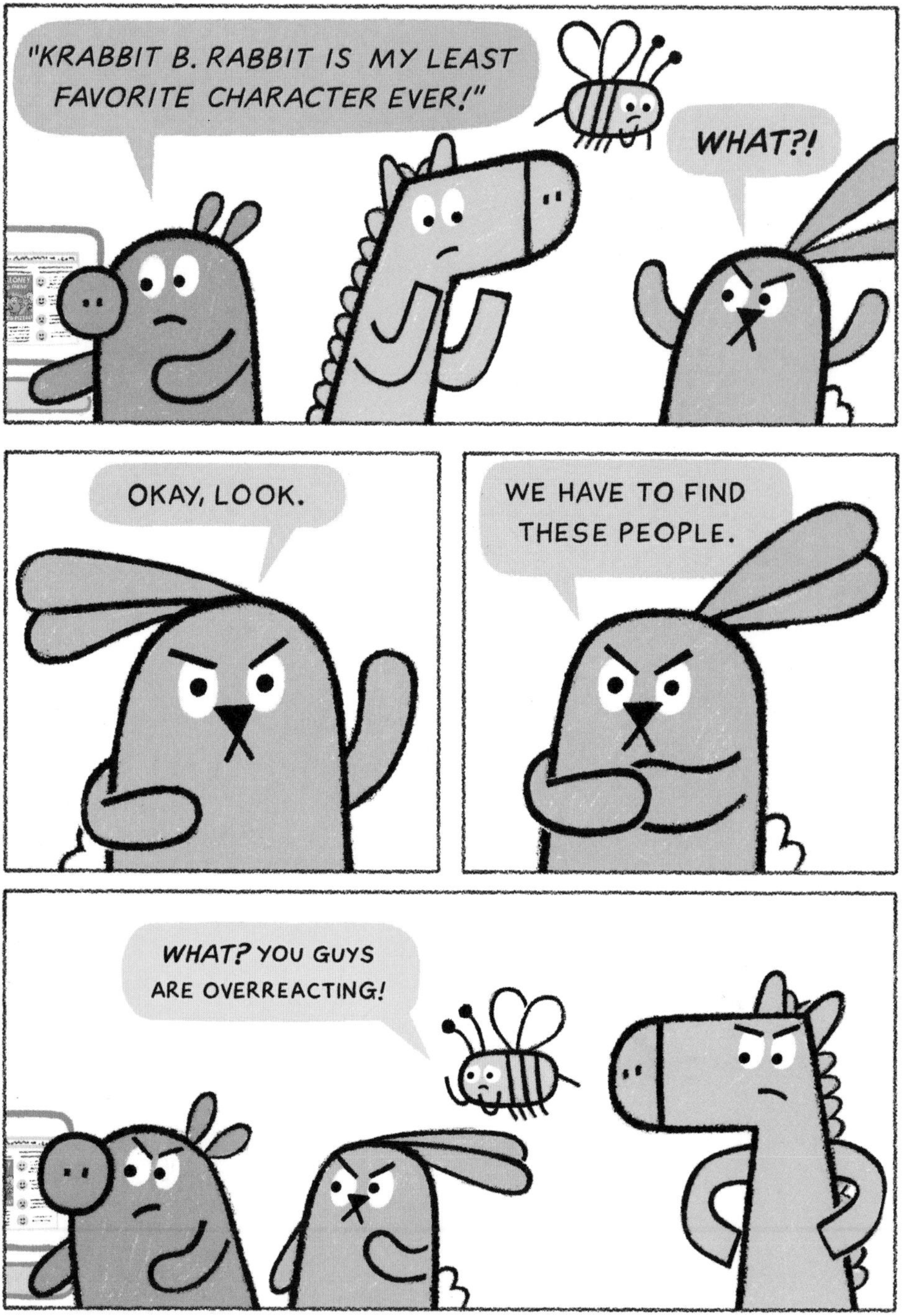
"KRABBIT B. RABBIT IS MY LEAST FAVORITE CHARACTER EVER!"
WHAT?!
OKAY, LOOK.
WE HAVE TO FIND THESE PEOPLE.
WHAT? YOU GUYS ARE OVERREACTING!

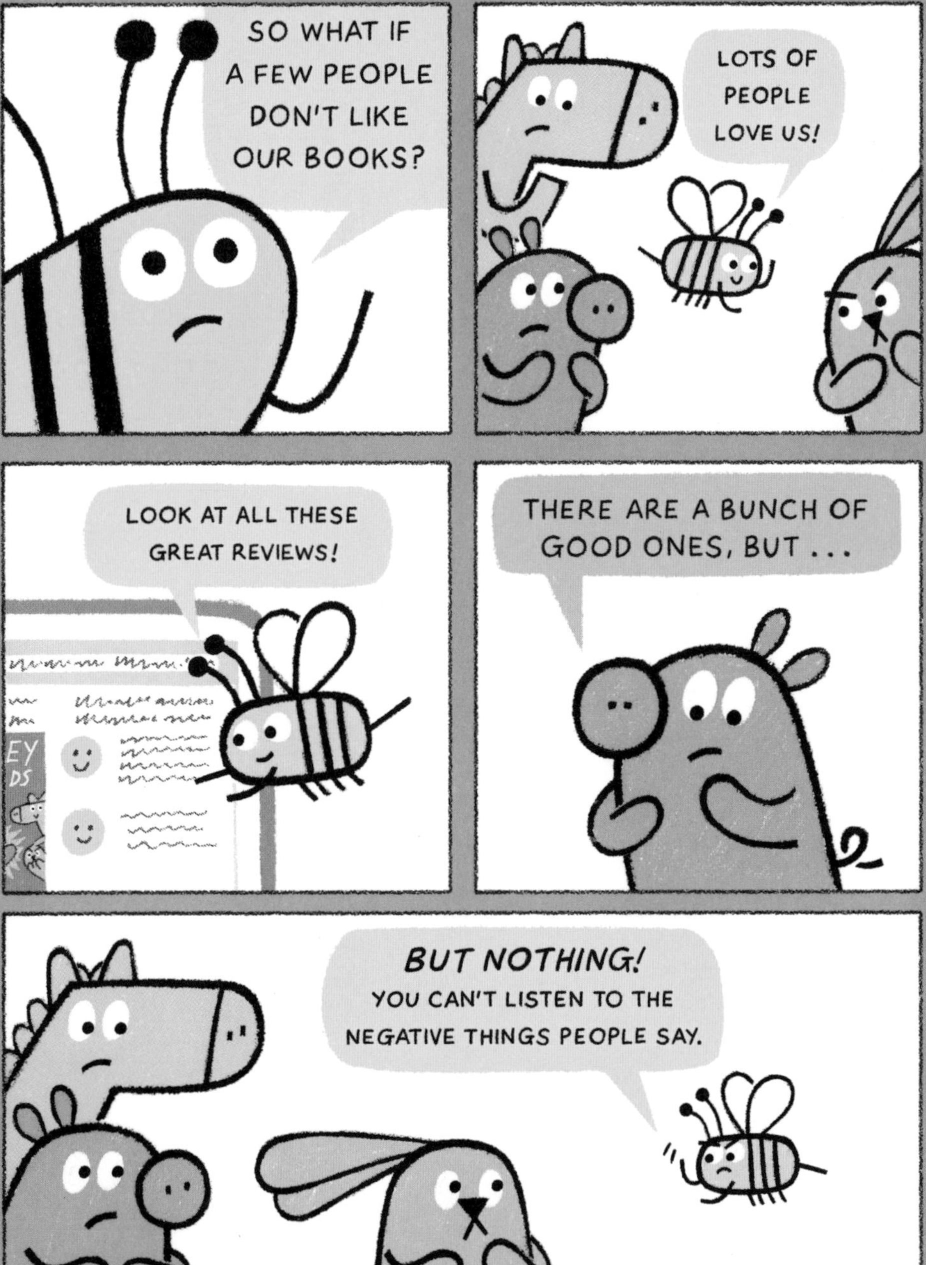
SO WHAT IF A FEW PEOPLE DON'T LIKE OUR BOOKS?
LOTS OF PEOPLE LOVE US!
LOOK AT ALL THESE GREAT REVIEWS!
THERE ARE A BUNCH OF GOOD ONES, BUT . . .
BUT NOTHING! YOU CAN'T LISTEN TO THE NEGATIVE THINGS PEOPLE SAY.

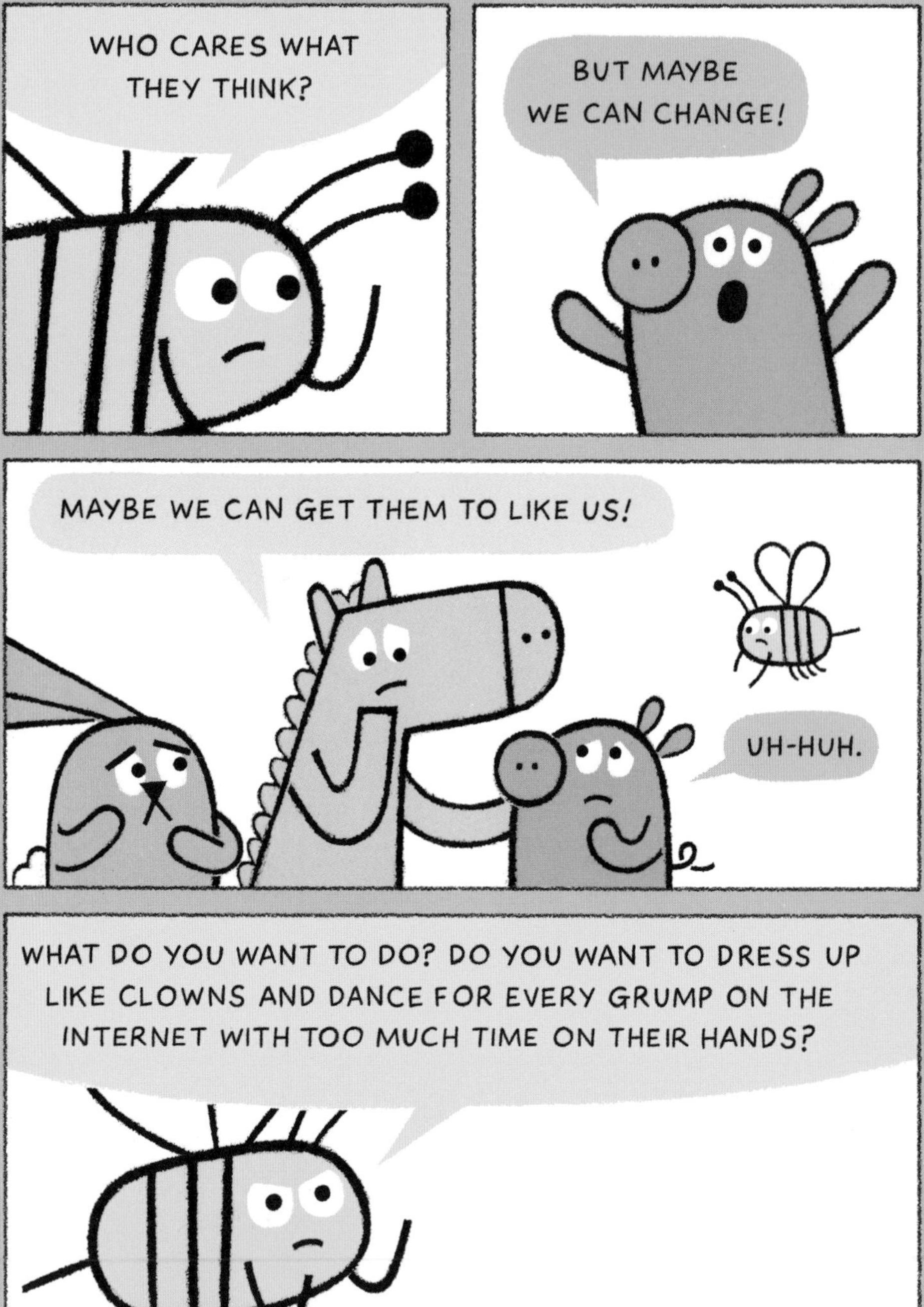
WHO CARES WHAT THEY THINK?
BUT MAYBE WE CAN CHANGE!
MAYBE WE CAN GET THEM TO LIKE US!
UH-HUH.
WHAT DO YOU WANT TO DO? DO YOU WANT TO DRESS UP LIKE CLOWNS AND DANCE FOR EVERY GRUMP ON THE INTERNET WITH TOO MUCH TIME ON THEIR HANDS?

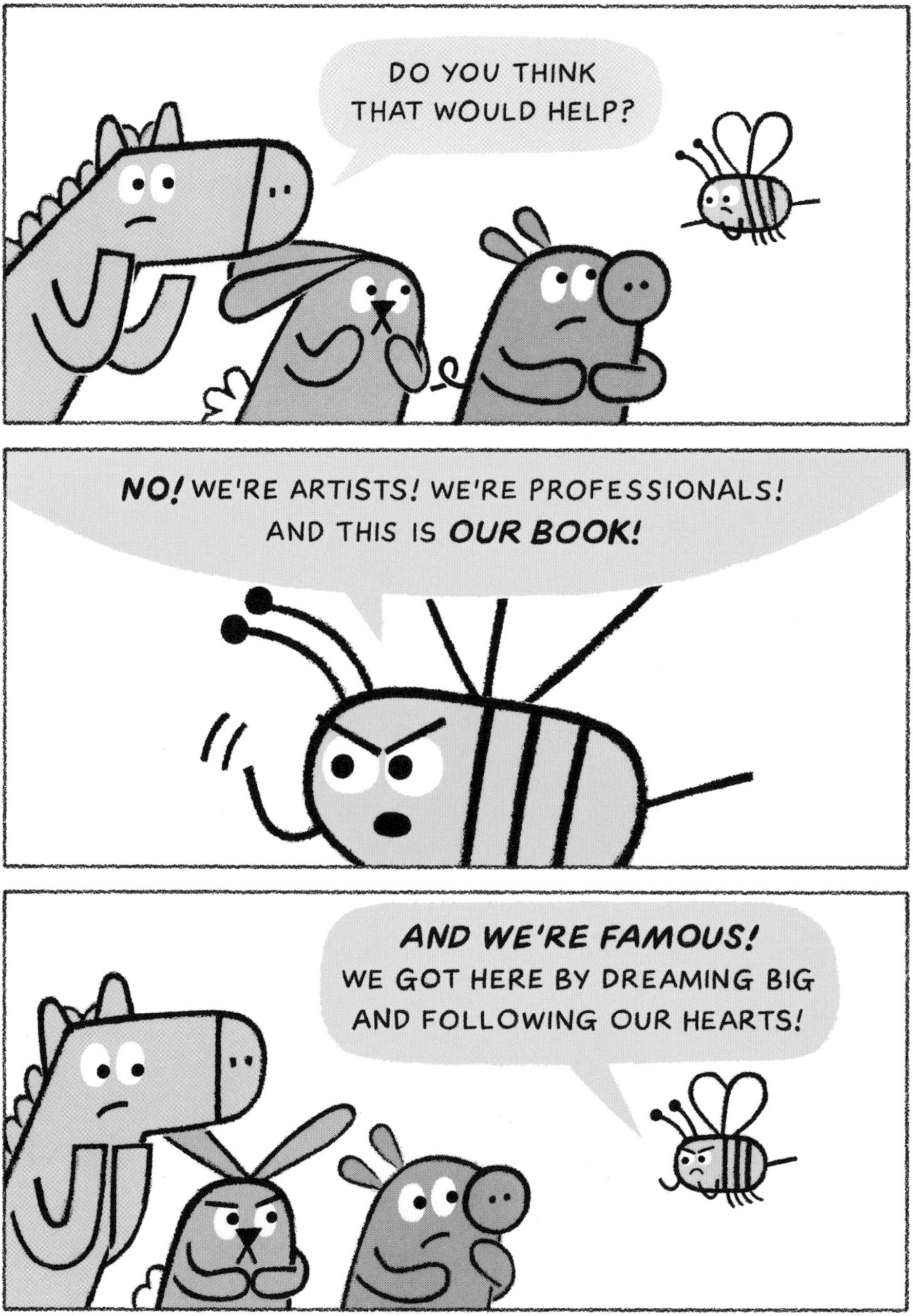
DO YOU THINK THAT WOULD HELP?
NO! WE'RE ARTISTS! WE'RE PROFESSIONALS! AND THIS IS OUR BOOK!
AND WE'RE FAMOUS! WE GOT HERE BY DREAMING BIG AND FOLLOWING OUR HEARTS!

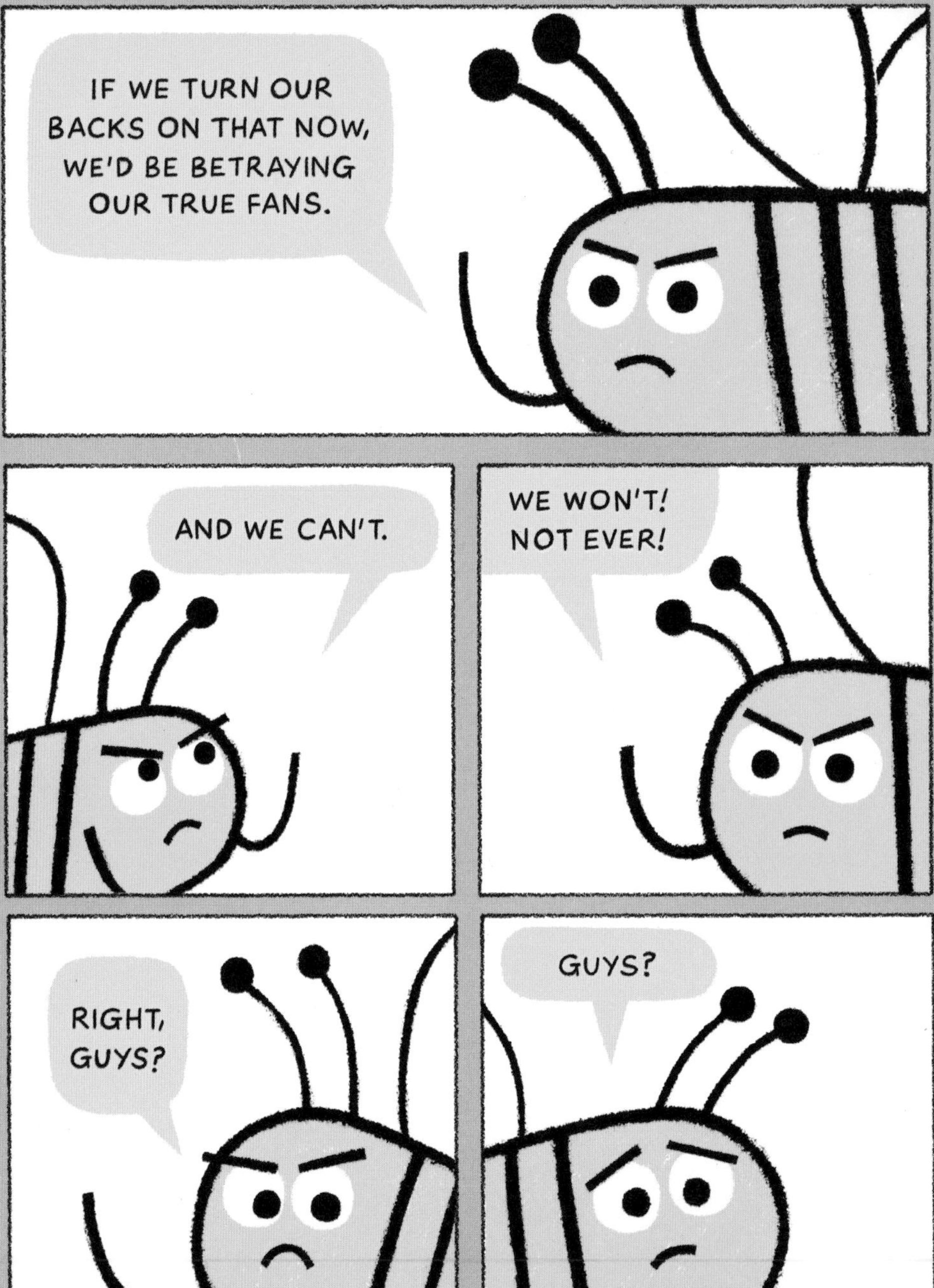
IF WE TURN OUR BACKS ON THAT NOW, WE'D BE BETRAYING OUR TRUE FANS.
AND WE CAN'T.
WE WON'T! NOT EVER!
RIGHT, GUYS?
GUYS?

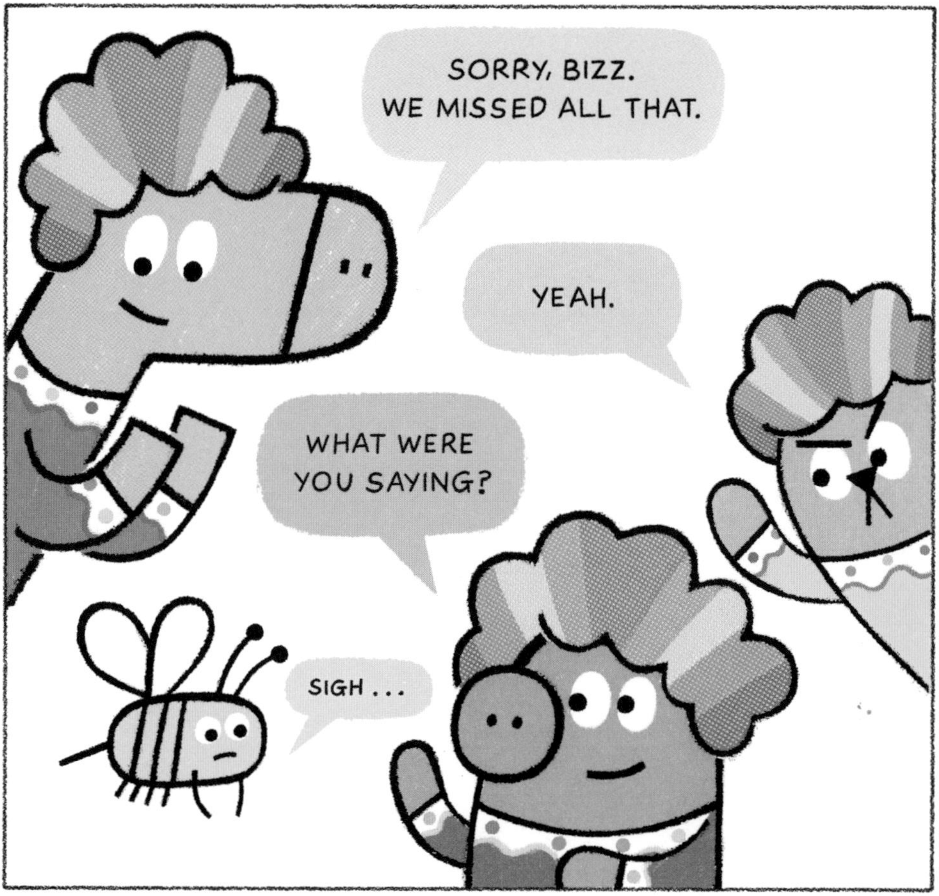
SORRY, BIZZ.
WE MISSED ALL THAT.
YEAH.
WHAT WERE YOU SAYING?
SIGH . . .

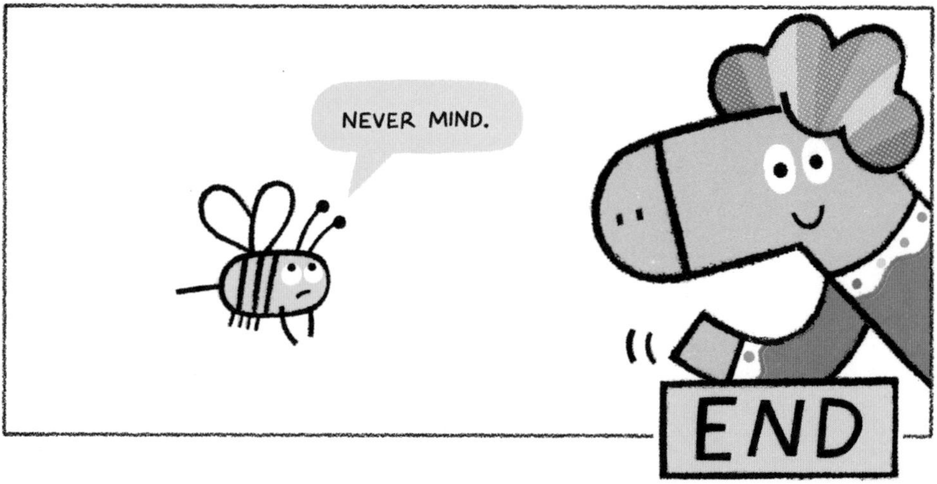
NEVER MIND.
END

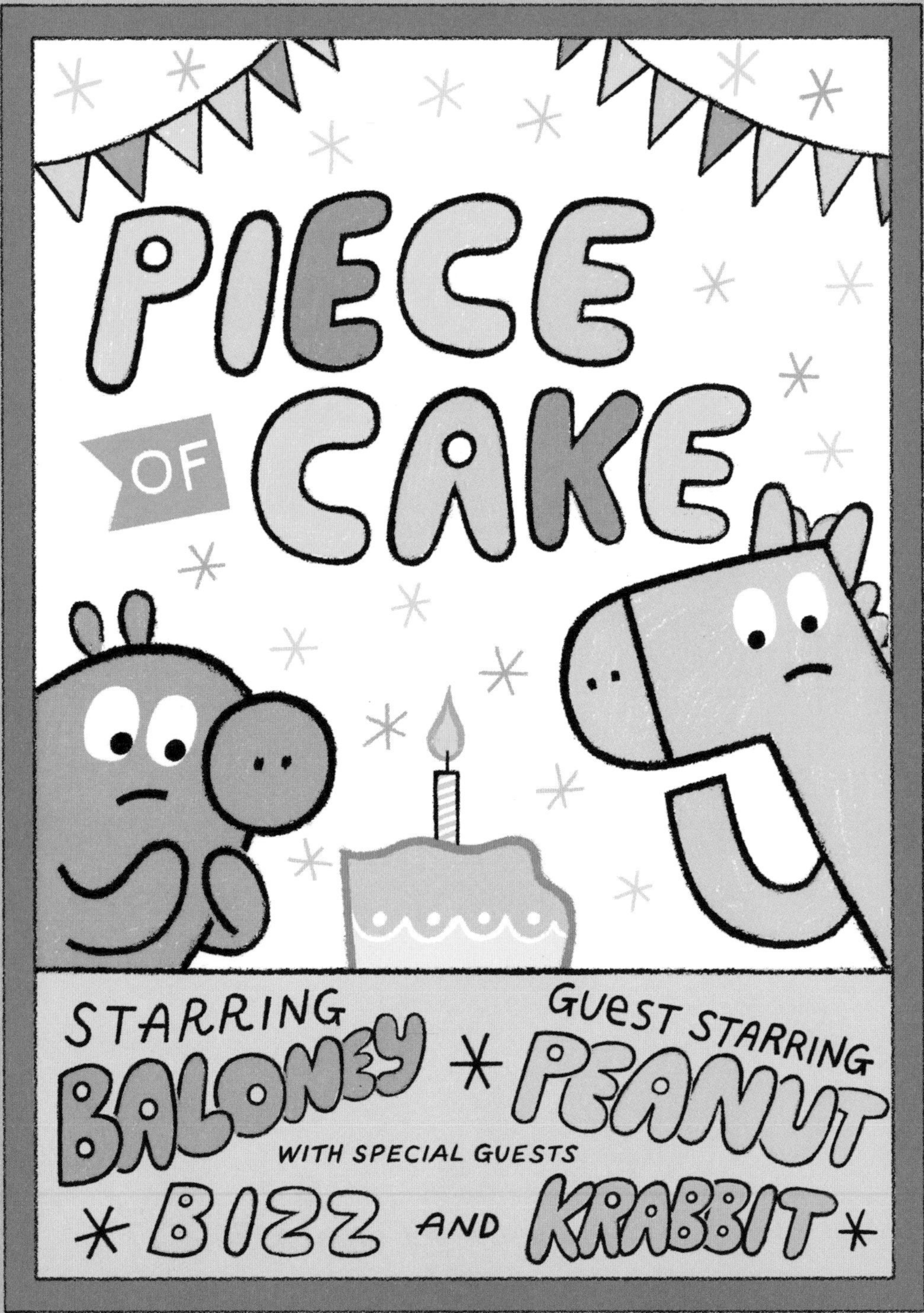
PIECE OF CAKE
STARRING BALONEY
GUEST STARRING PEANUT
WITH SPECIAL GUESTS
BIZZ AND KRABBIT

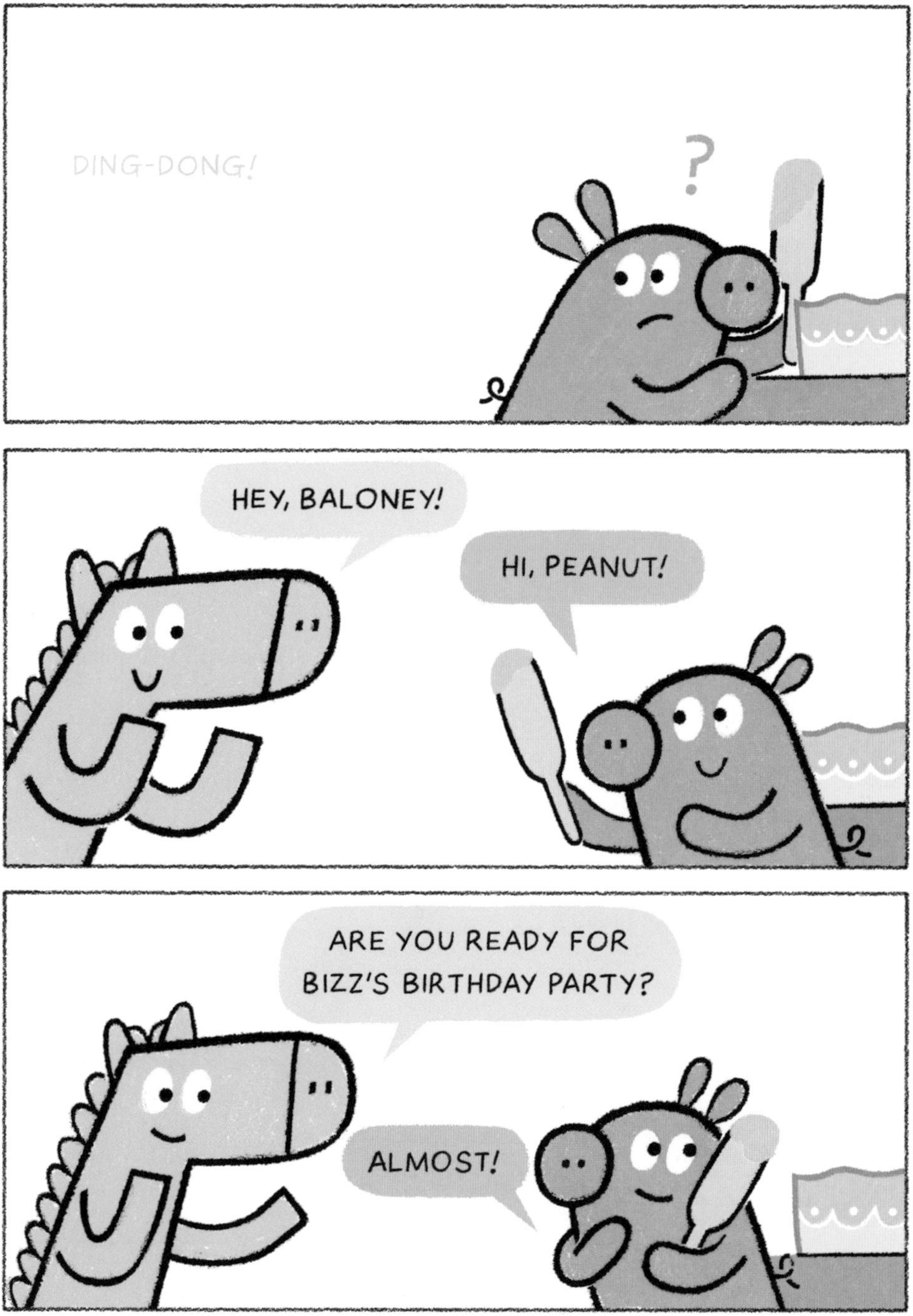
DING-DONG!
?
HEY, BALONEY!
HI, PEANUT!
ARE YOU READY FOR BIZZ'S BIRTHDAY PARTY?
ALMOST!

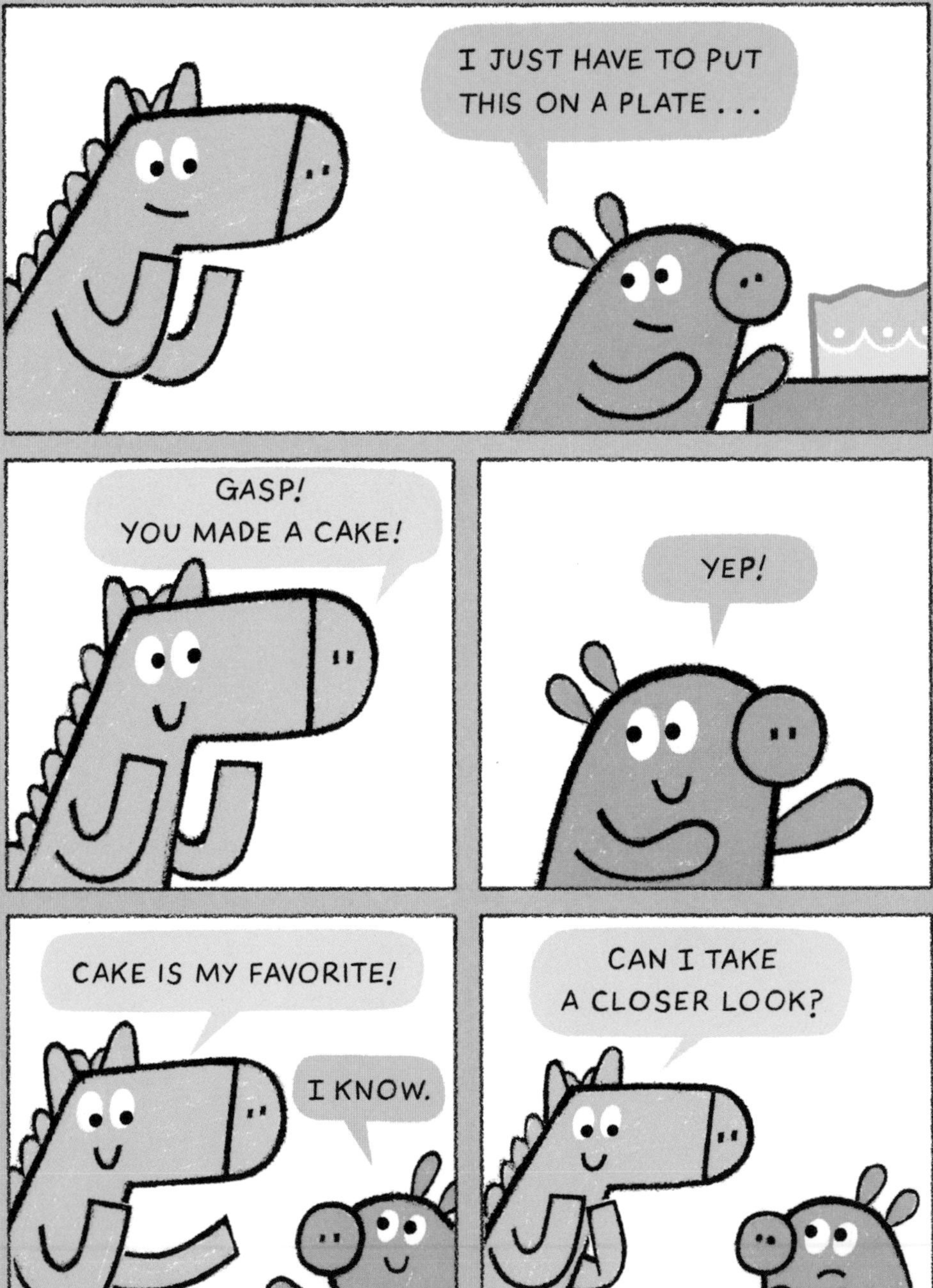
I JUST HAVE TO PUT THIS ON A PLATE . . .
GASP! YOU MADE A CAKE!
YEP!
CAKE IS MY FAVORITE!
I KNOW.
CAN I TAKE A CLOSER LOOK?

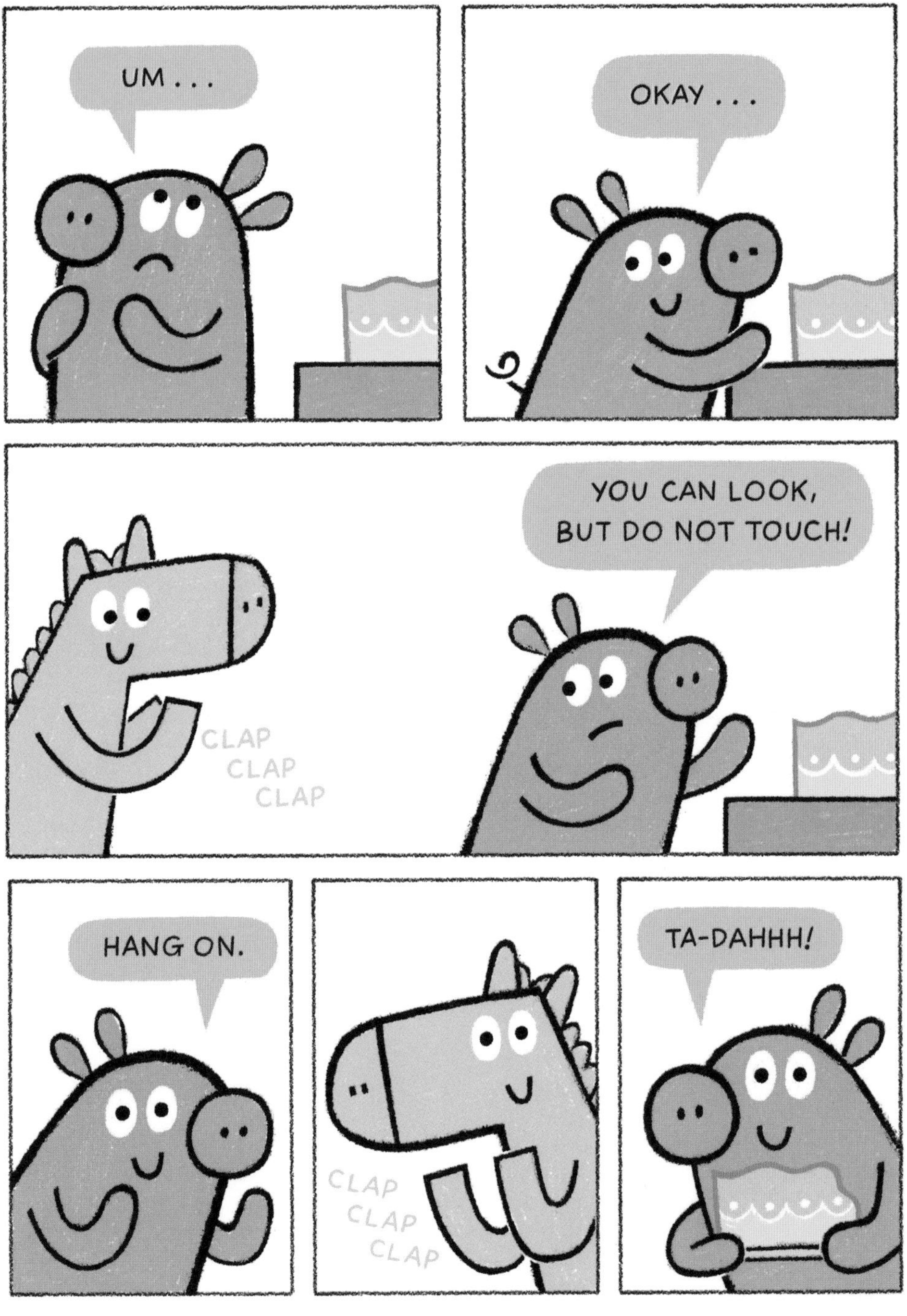
UM . . .
OKAY . . .
YOU CAN LOOK, BUT DO NOT TOUCH!
CLAP CLAP CLAP
HANG ON.
CLAP CLAP CLAP
TA-DAHHH!

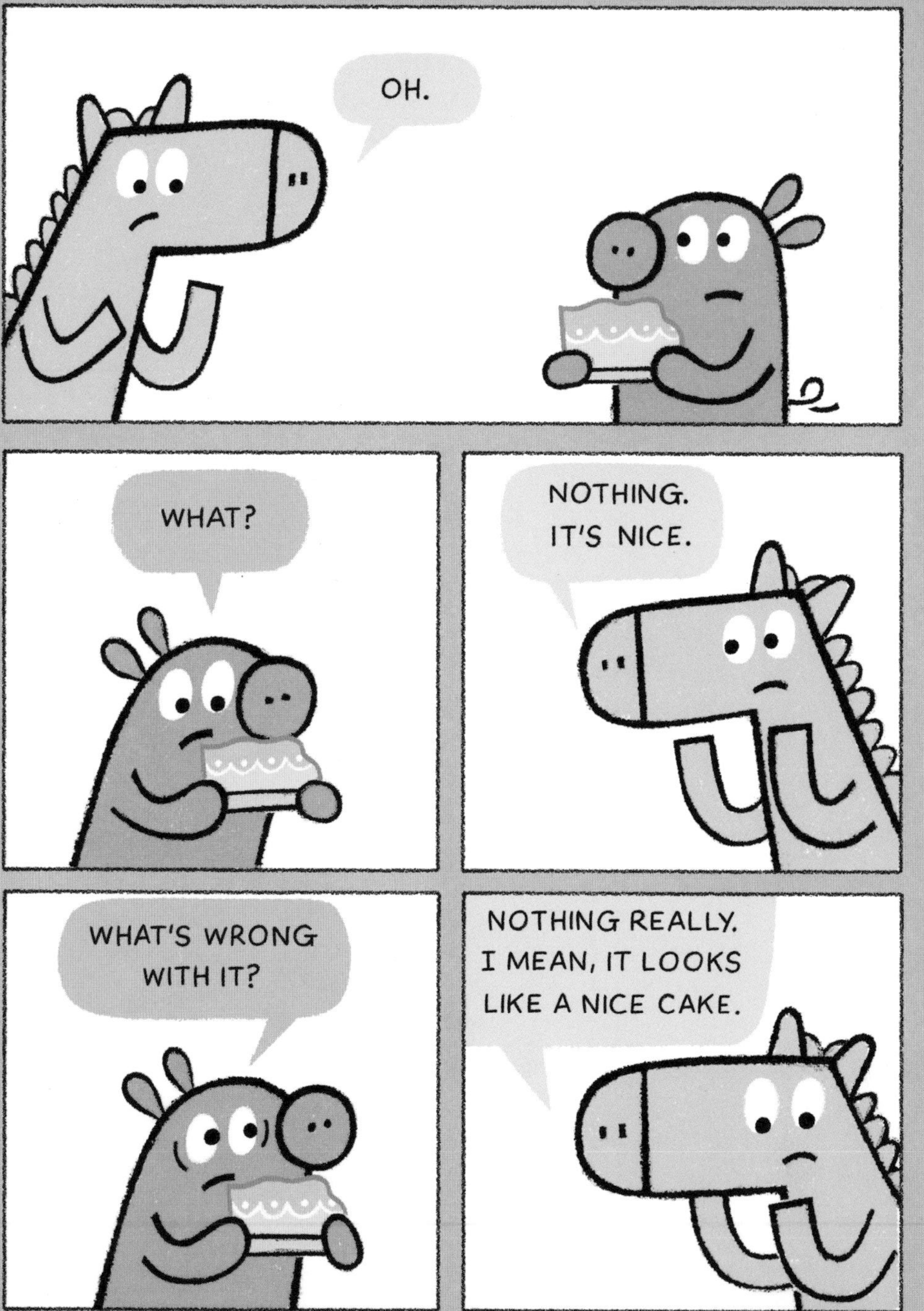
OH.
WHAT?
NOTHING. IT'S NICE.
WHAT'S WRONG WITH IT?
NOTHING REALLY. I MEAN, IT LOOKS LIKE A NICE CAKE.

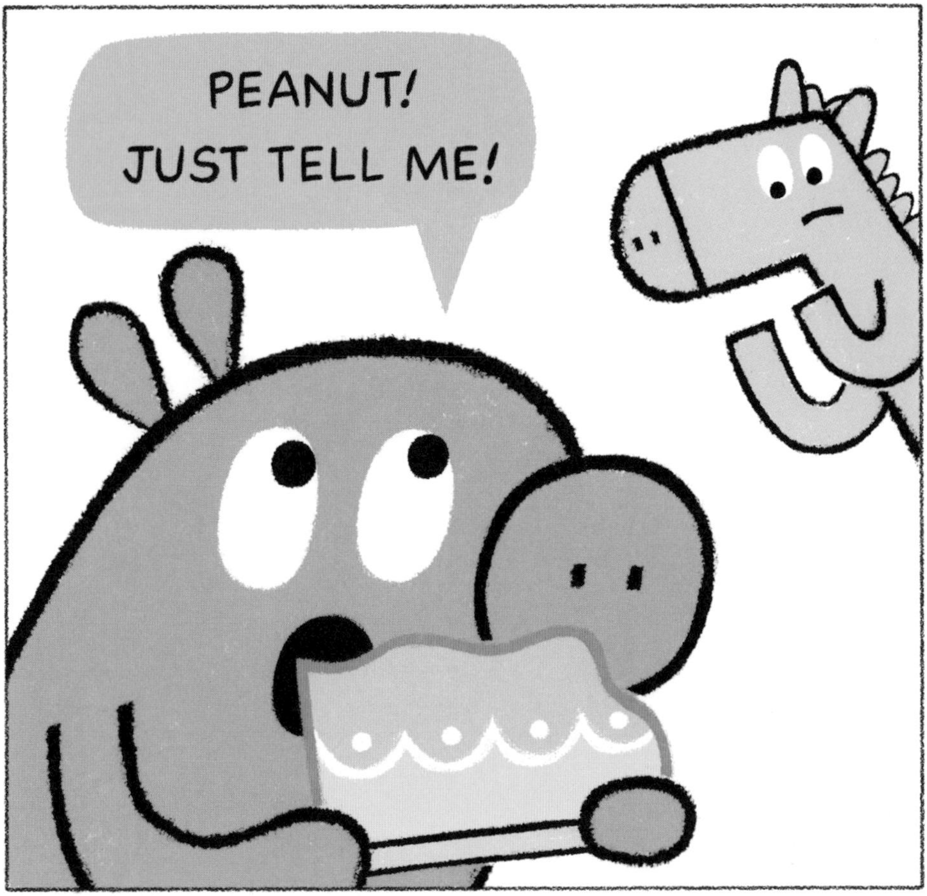
PEANUT! JUST TELL ME!

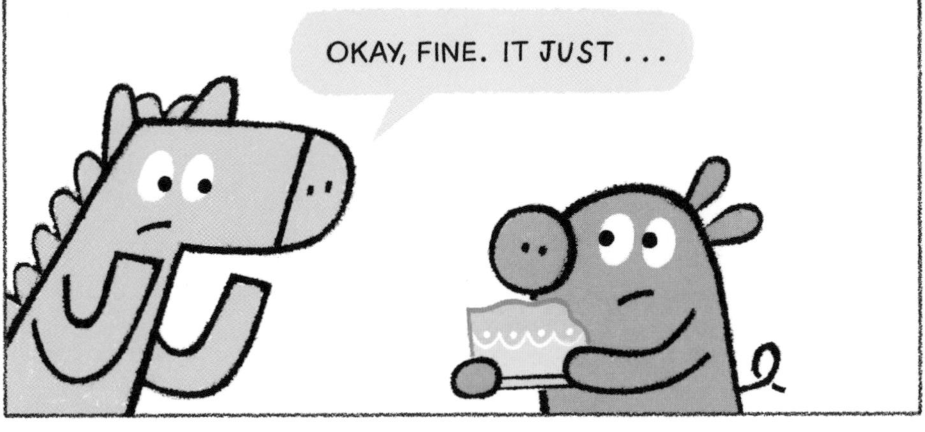
OKAY, FINE. IT JUST . . .

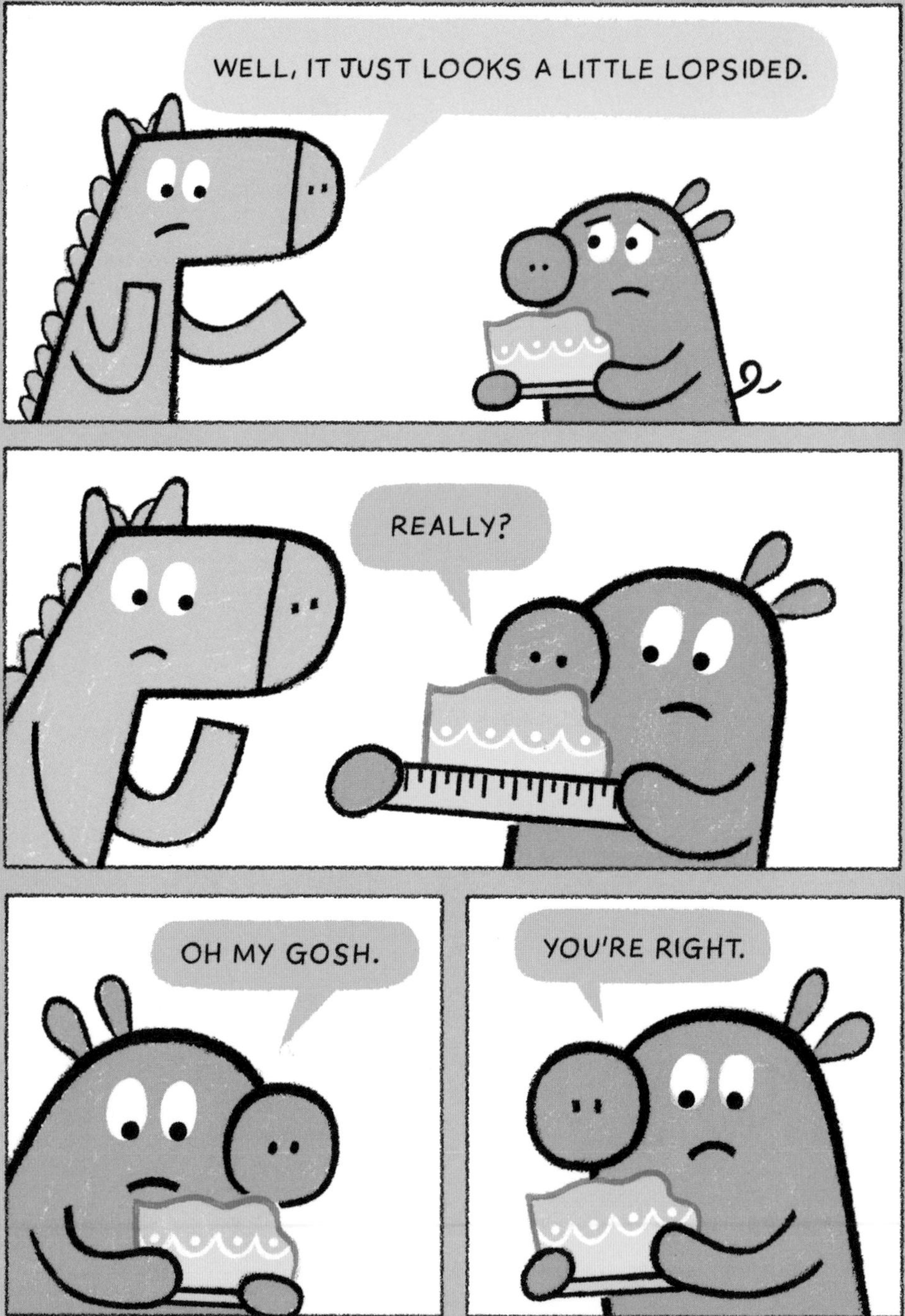
WELL, IT JUST LOOKS A LITTLE LOPSIDED.
REALLY?
OH MY GOSH.
YOU'RE RIGHT.

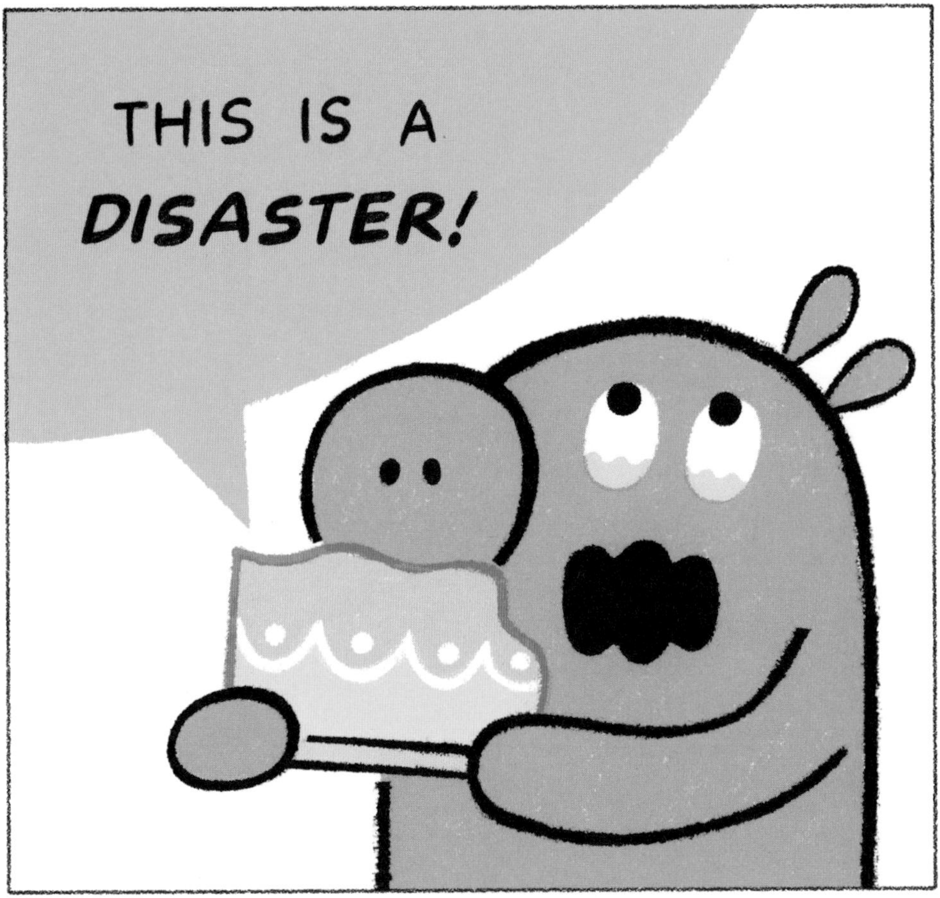
THIS IS A *DISASTER!*

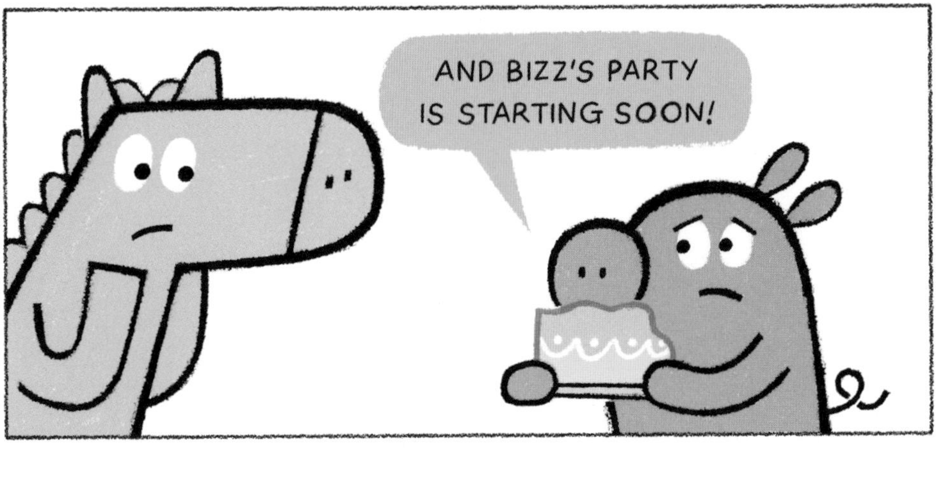
AND BIZZ'S PARTY IS STARTING SOON!

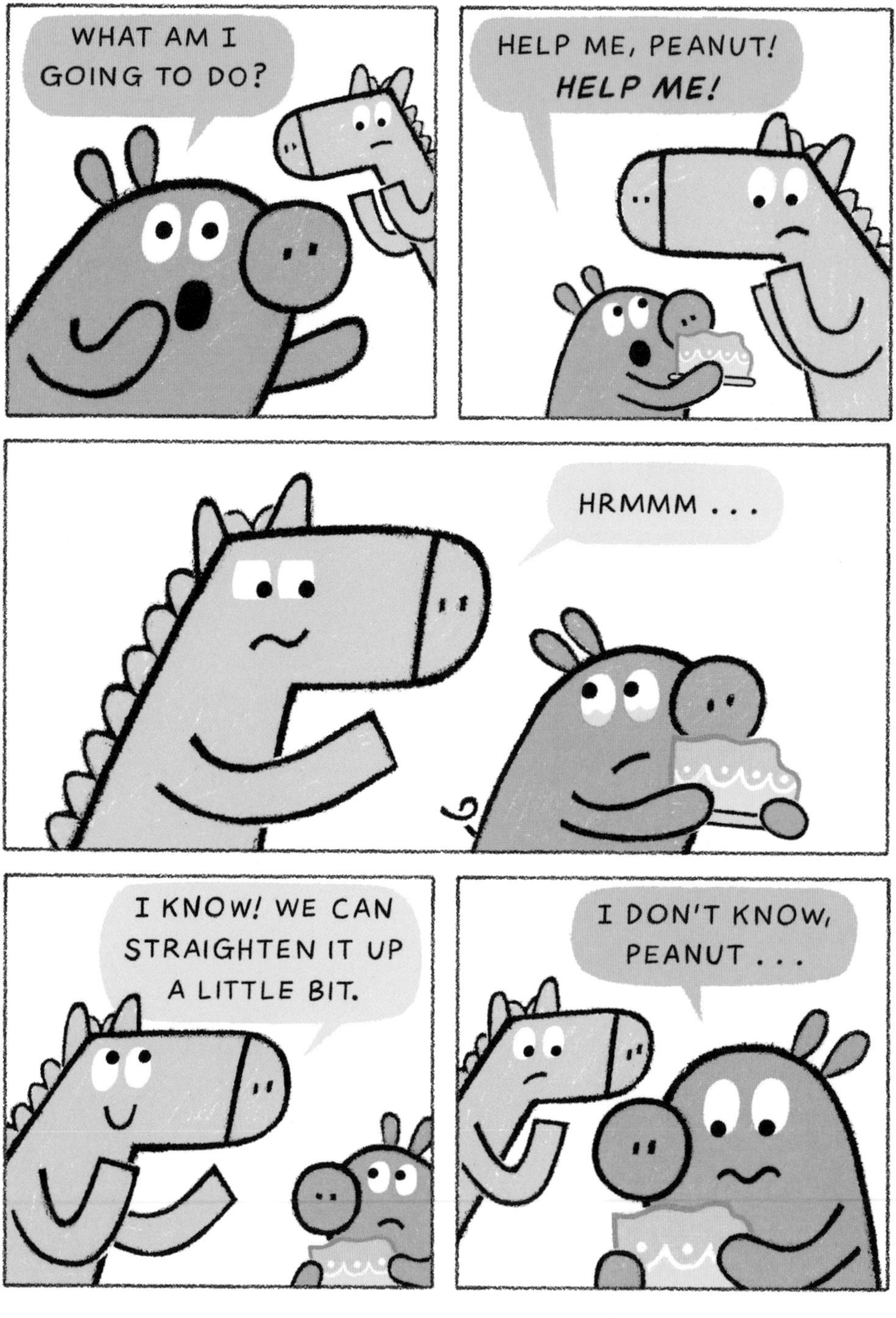
WHAT AM I GOING TO DO?
HELP ME, PEANUT! ***HELP ME!***
HRMMM . . .
I KNOW! WE CAN STRAIGHTEN IT UP A LITTLE BIT.
I DON'T KNOW, PEANUT . . .

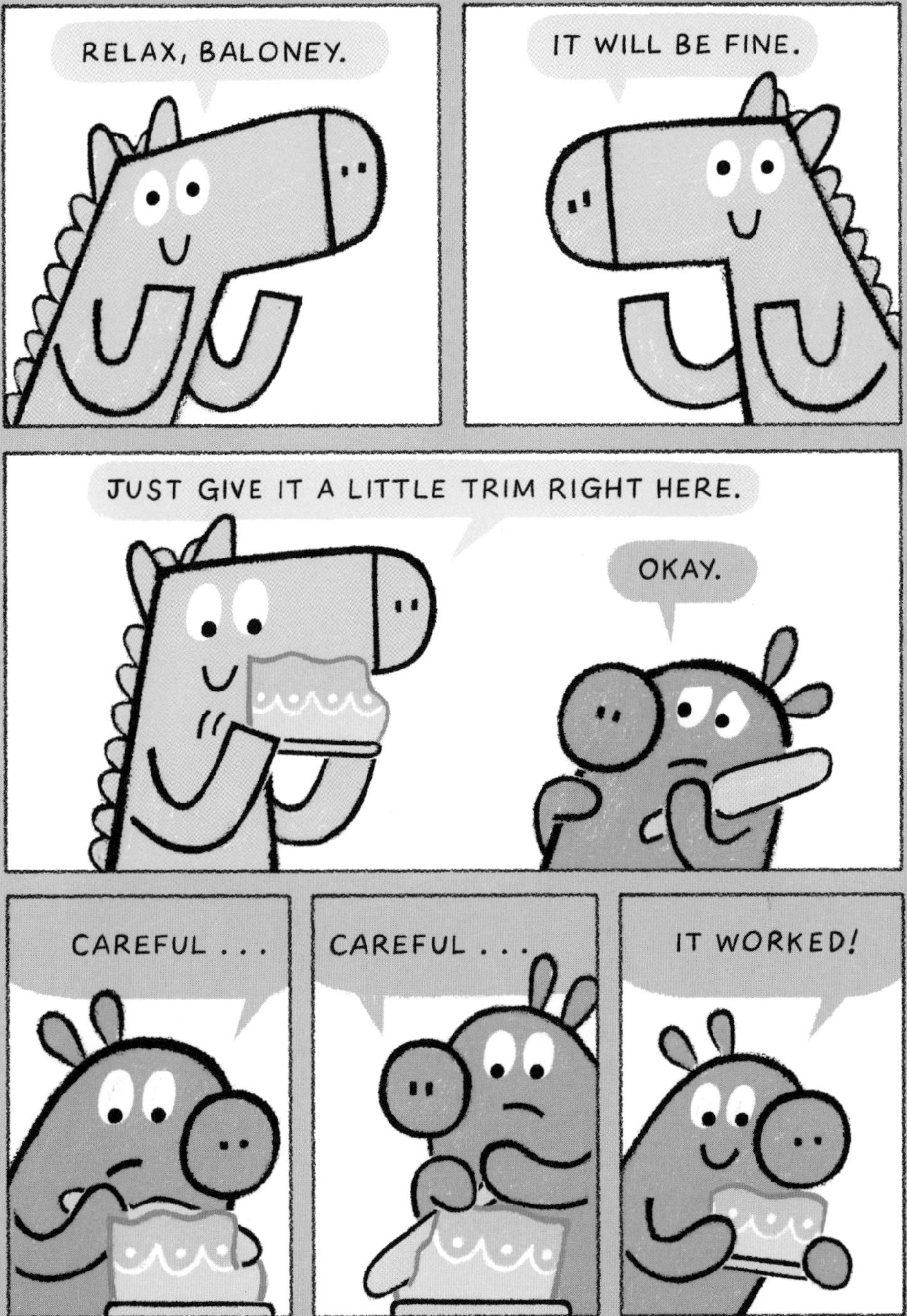
RELAX, BALONEY.
IT WILL BE FINE.
JUST GIVE IT A LITTLE TRIM RIGHT HERE.
OKAY.
CAREFUL . . .
CAREFUL . . .
IT WORKED!

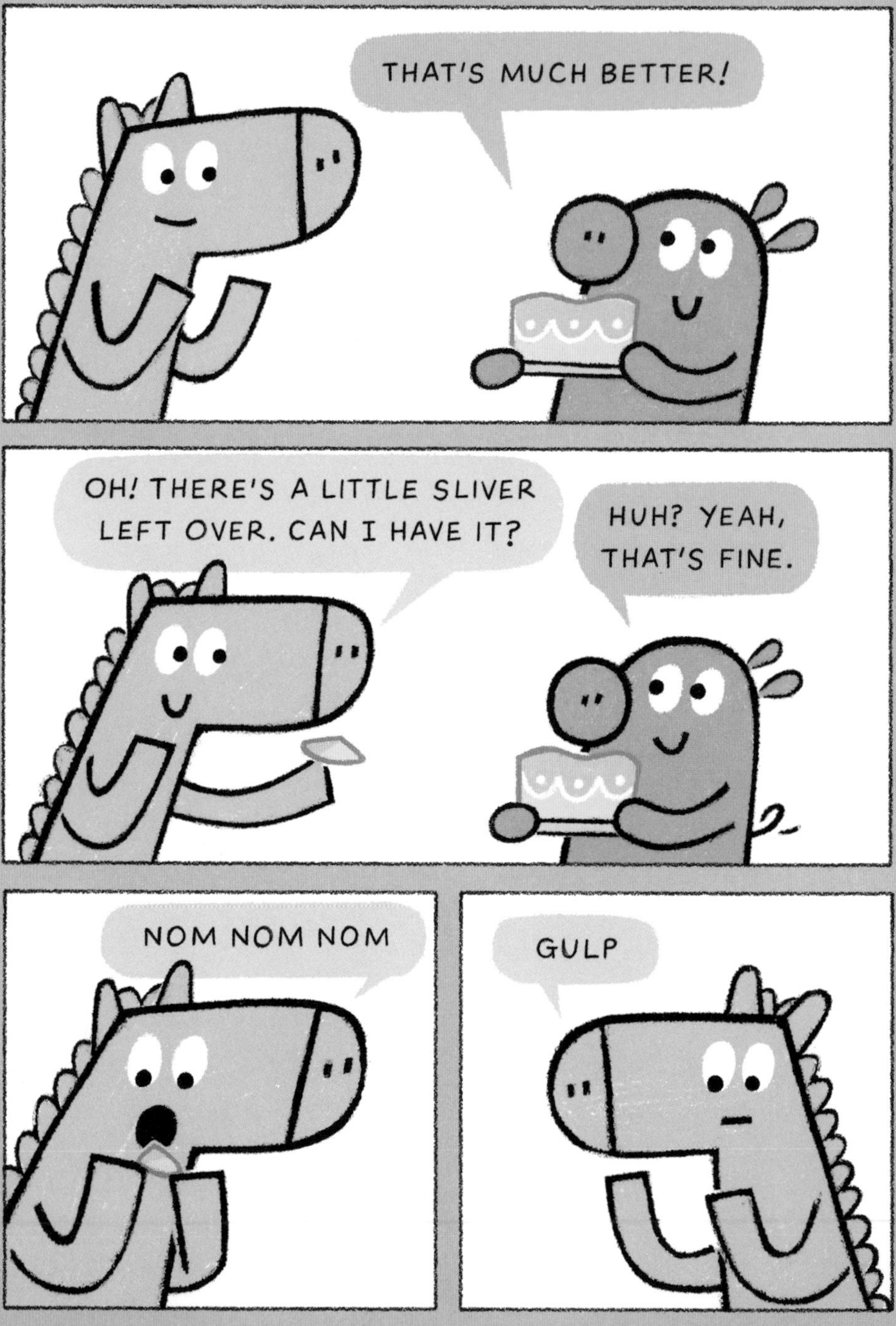
THAT'S MUCH BETTER!
OH! THERE'S A LITTLE SLIVER LEFT OVER. CAN I HAVE IT?
HUH? YEAH, THAT'S FINE.
NOM NOM NOM
GULP

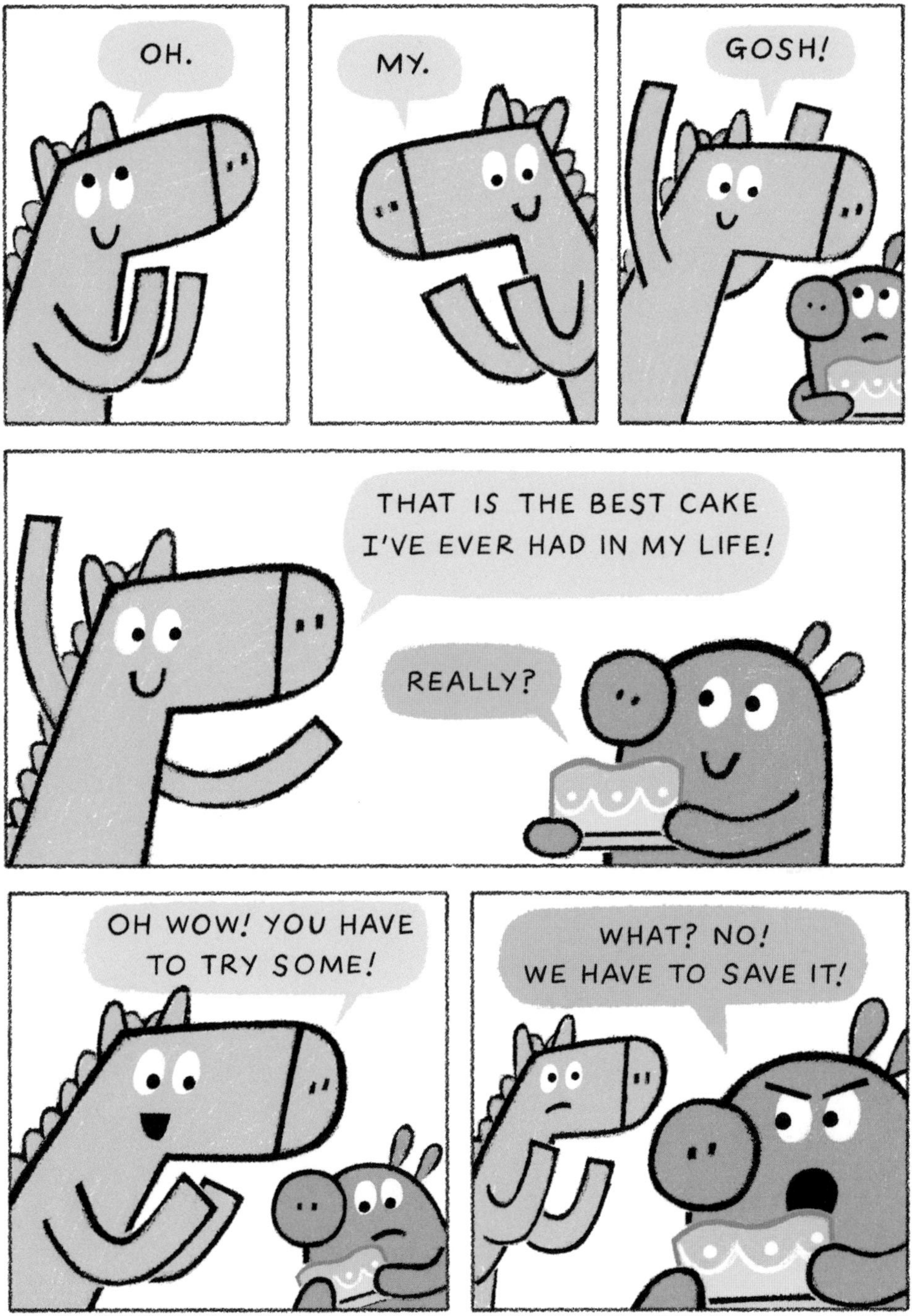
OH.
MY.
GOSH!
THAT IS THE BEST CAKE I'VE EVER HAD IN MY LIFE!
REALLY?
OH WOW! YOU HAVE TO TRY SOME!
WHAT? NO! WE HAVE TO SAVE IT!

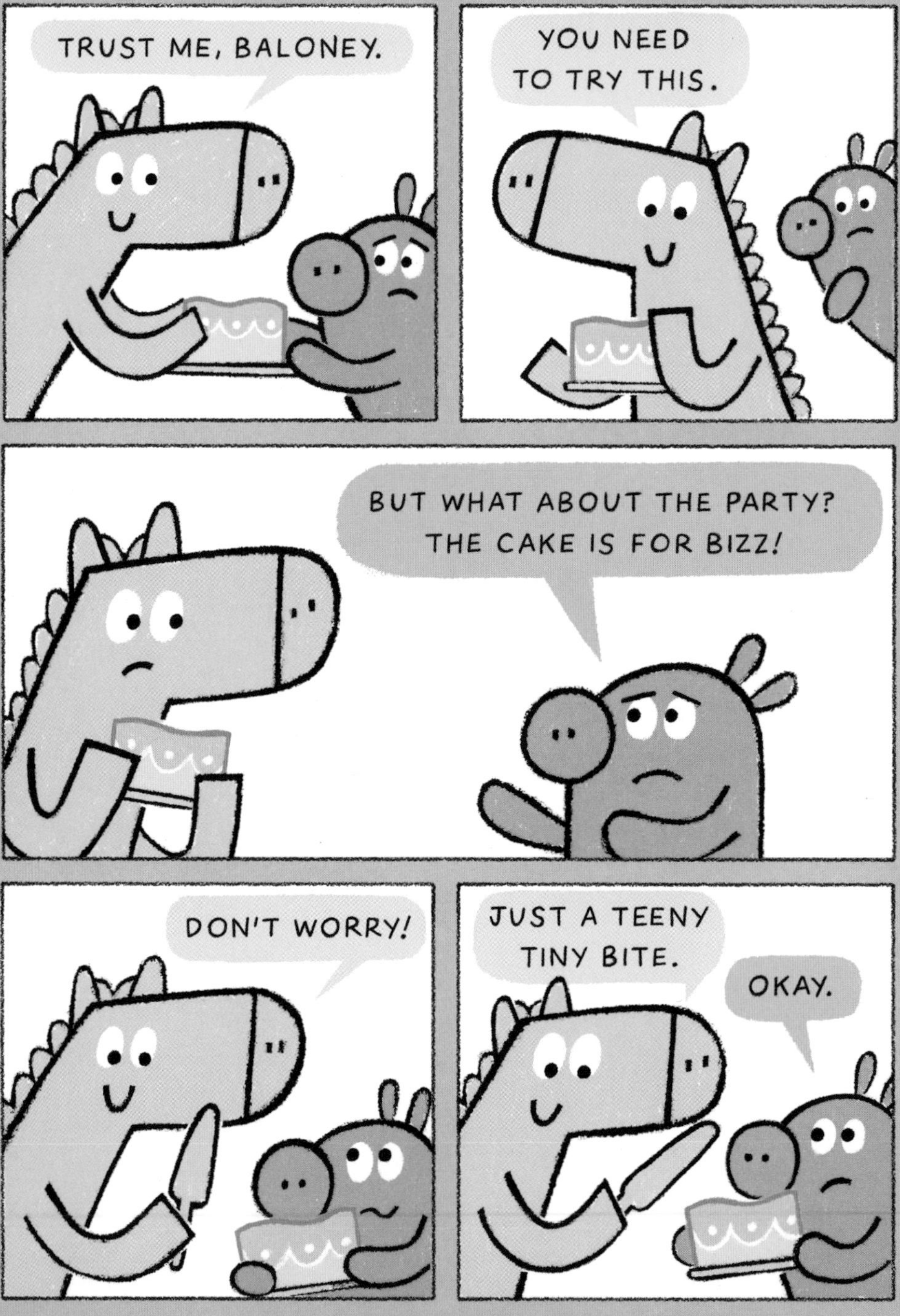
TRUST ME, BALONEY.
YOU NEED TO TRY THIS.
BUT WHAT ABOUT THE PARTY? THE CAKE IS FOR BIZZ!
DON'T WORRY!
JUST A TEENY TINY BITE.
OKAY.

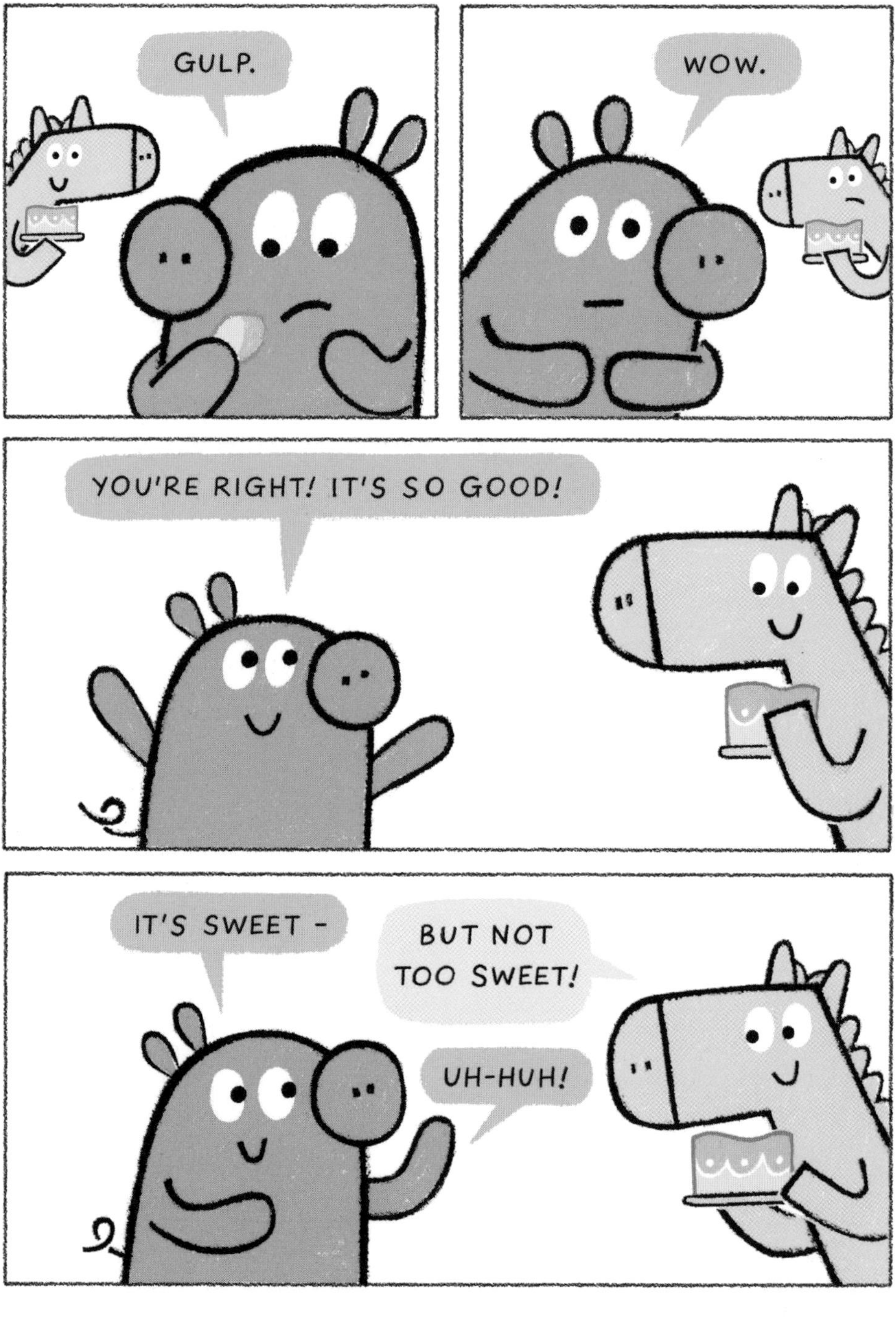
GULP.
WOW.
YOU'RE RIGHT! IT'S SO GOOD!
IT'S SWEET -
BUT NOT TOO SWEET!
UH-HUH!

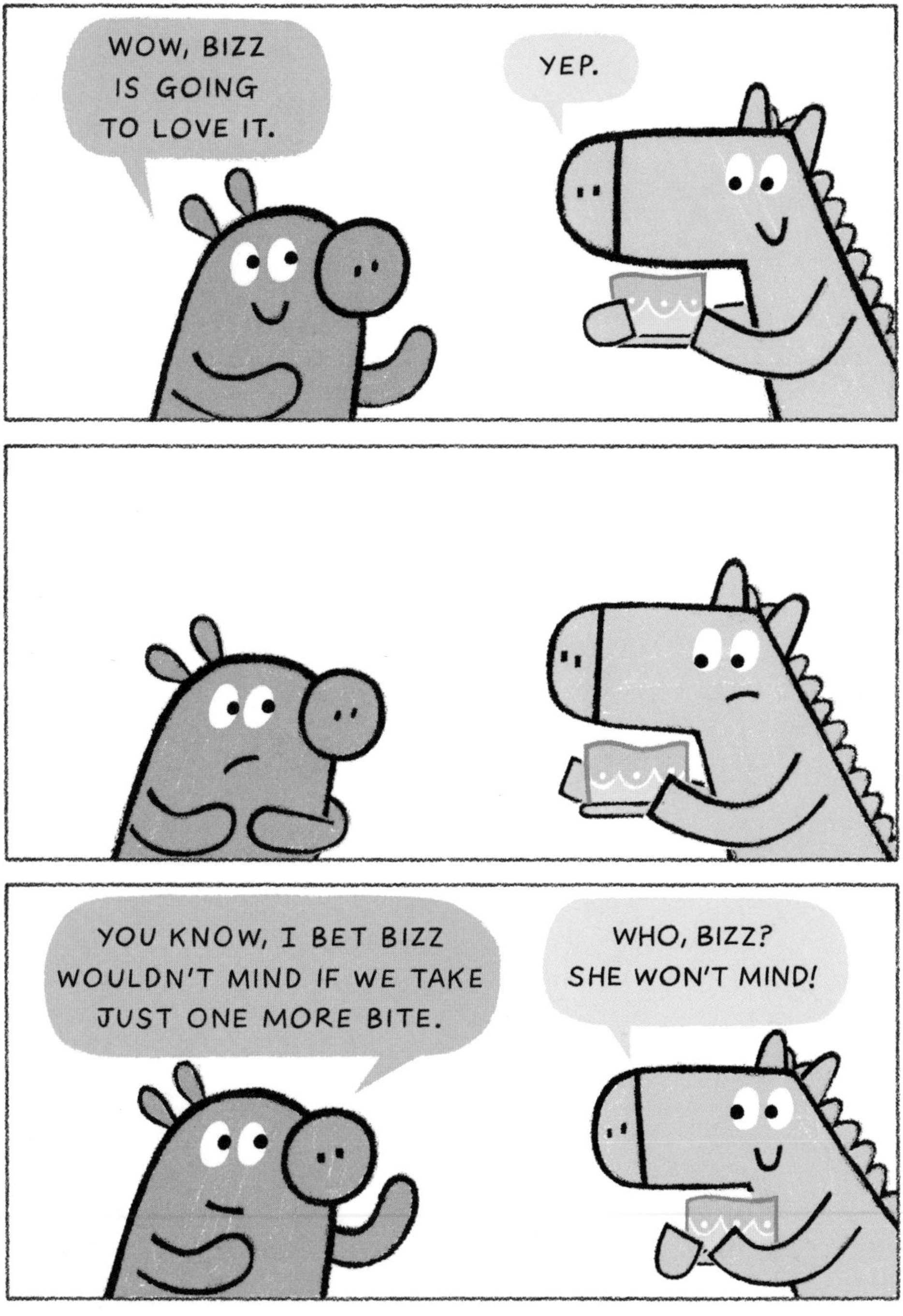
WOW, BIZZ IS GOING TO LOVE IT.
YEP.
YOU KNOW, I BET BIZZ WOULDN'T MIND IF WE TAKE JUST ONE MORE BITE.
WHO, BIZZ? SHE WON'T MIND!

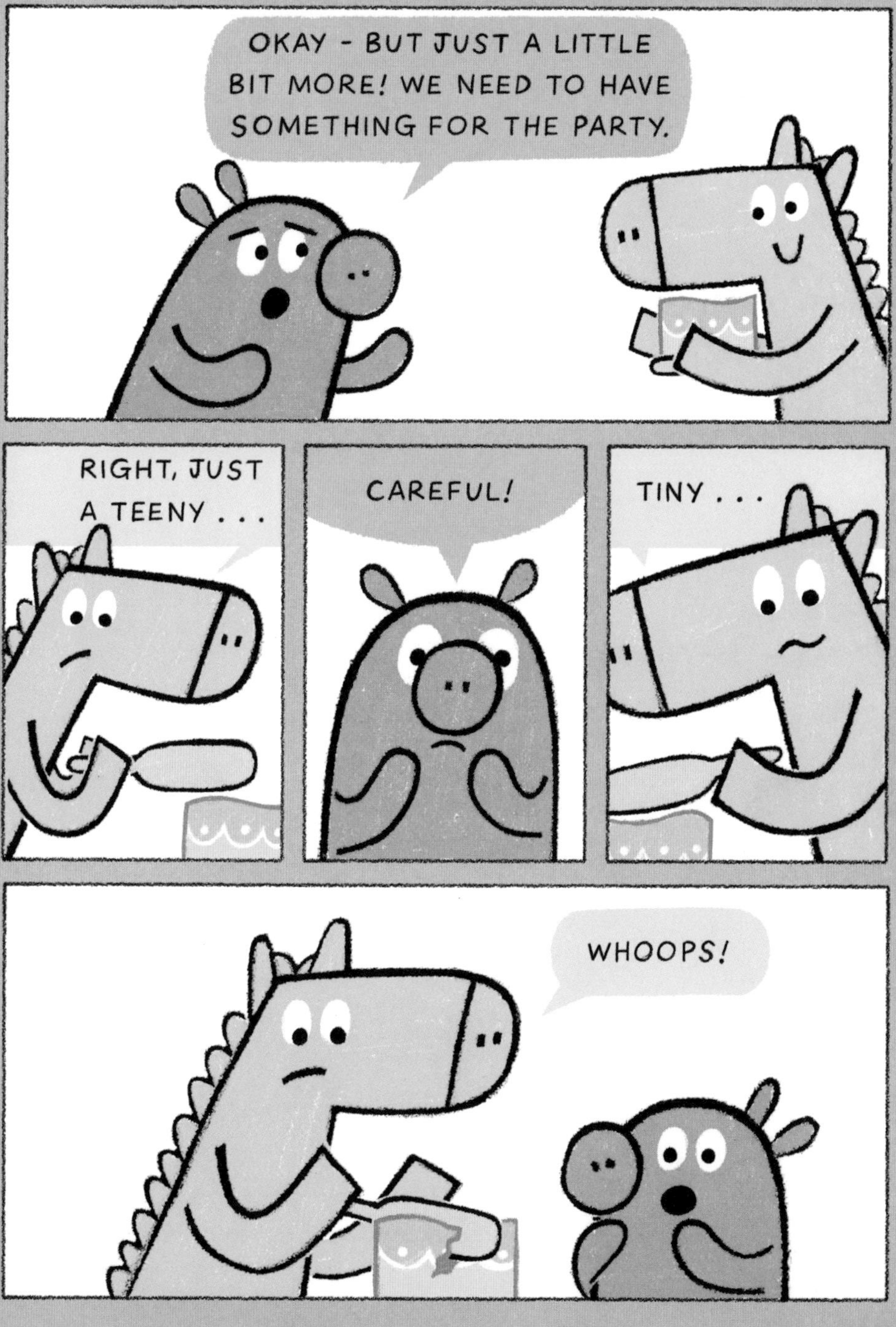
OKAY - BUT JUST A LITTLE BIT MORE! WE NEED TO HAVE SOMETHING FOR THE PARTY.
RIGHT, JUST A TEENY . . .
CAREFUL!
TINY . . .
WHOOPS!

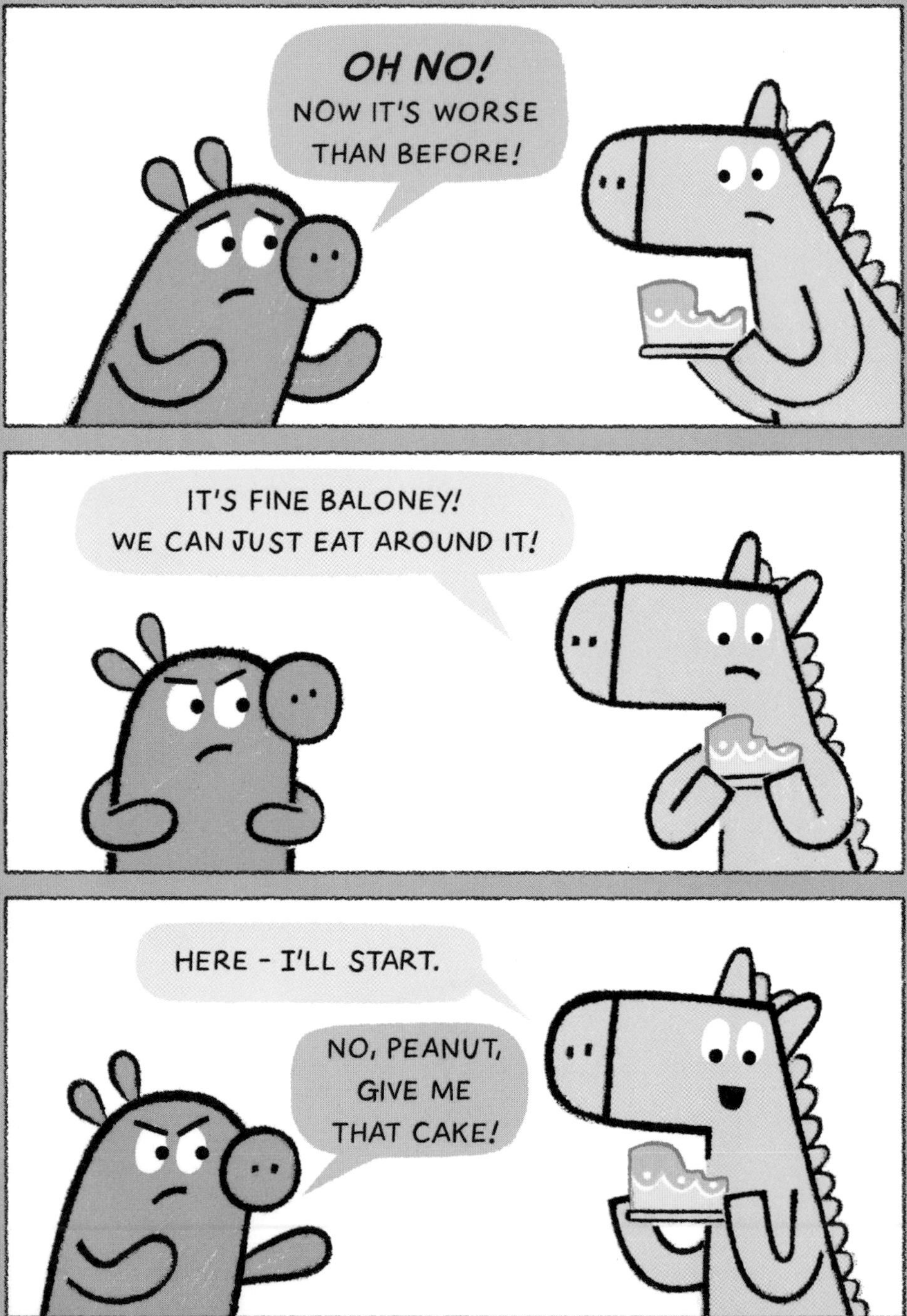
OH NO! NOW IT'S WORSE THAN BEFORE!
IT'S FINE BALONEY! WE CAN JUST EAT AROUND IT!
HERE - I'LL START.
NO, PEANUT, GIVE ME THAT CAKE!

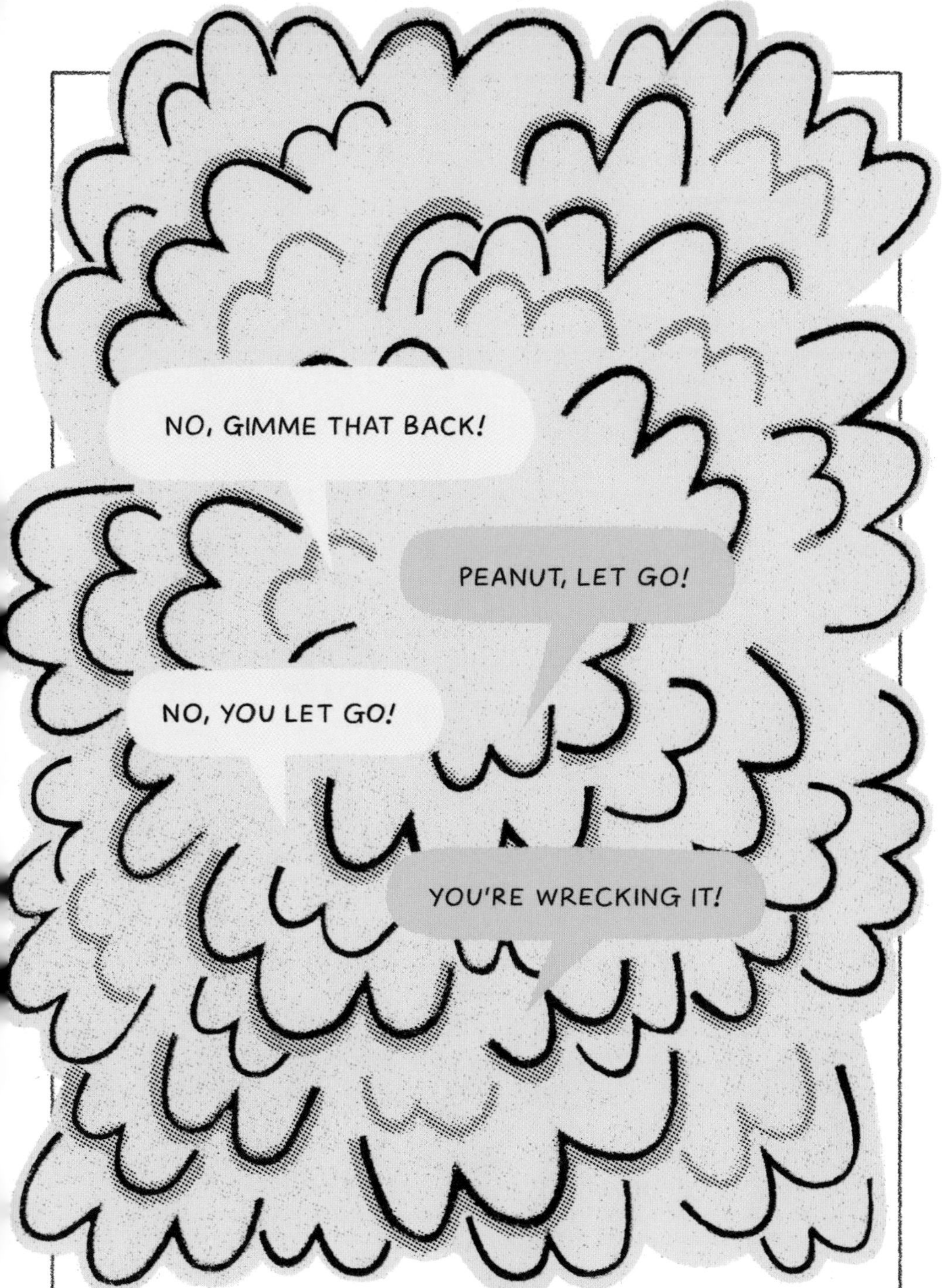
NO, GIMME THAT BACK!
PEANUT, LET GO!
NO, YOU LET GO!
YOU'RE WRECKING IT!

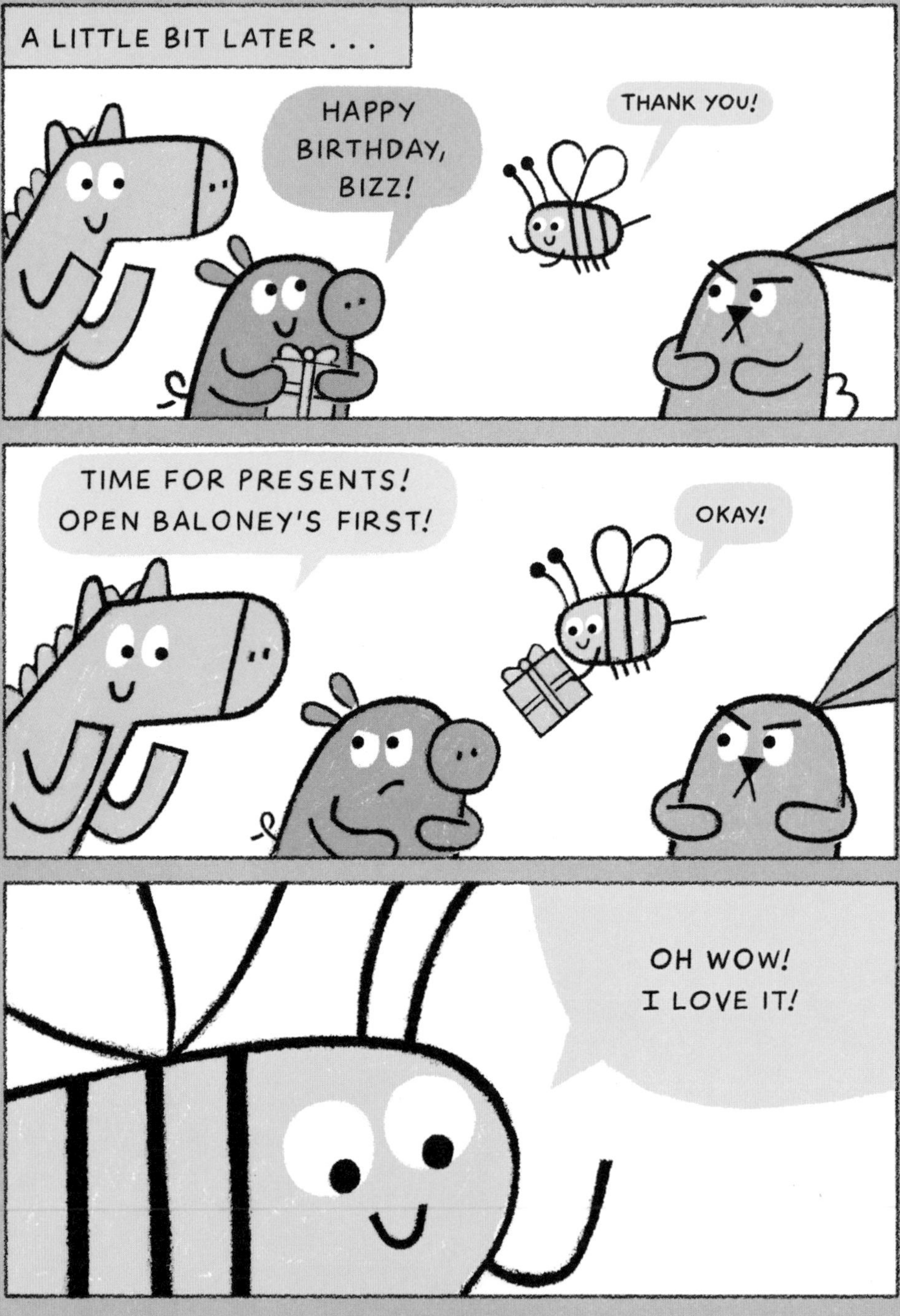
A LITTLE BIT LATER . . .
HAPPY BIRTHDAY, BIZZ!
THANK YOU!
TIME FOR PRESENTS! OPEN BALONEY'S FIRST!
OKAY!
OH WOW! I LOVE IT!

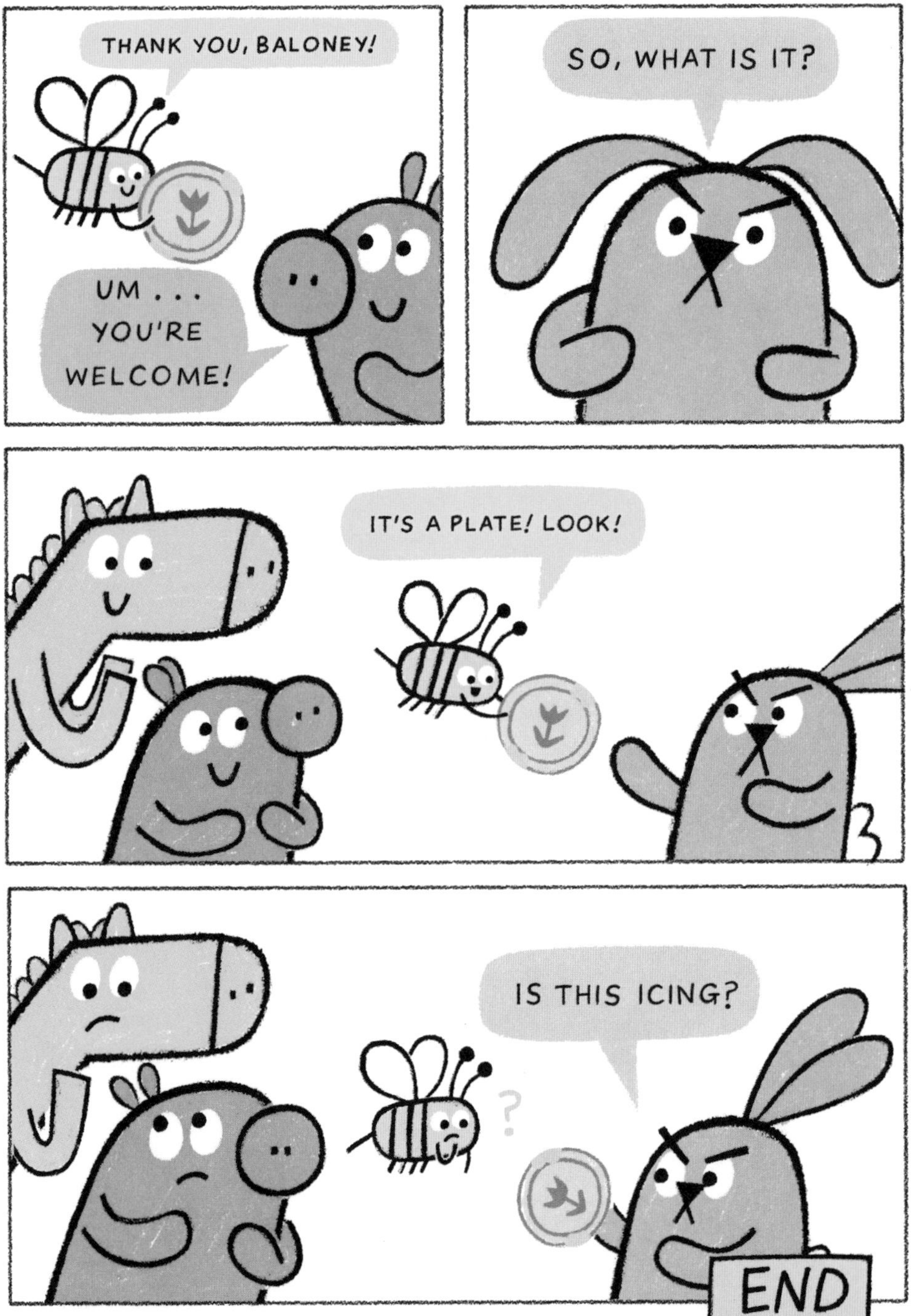
THANK YOU, BALONEY!
UM . . . YOU'RE WELCOME!
SO, WHAT IS IT?
IT'S A PLATE! LOOK!
IS THIS ICING?
END

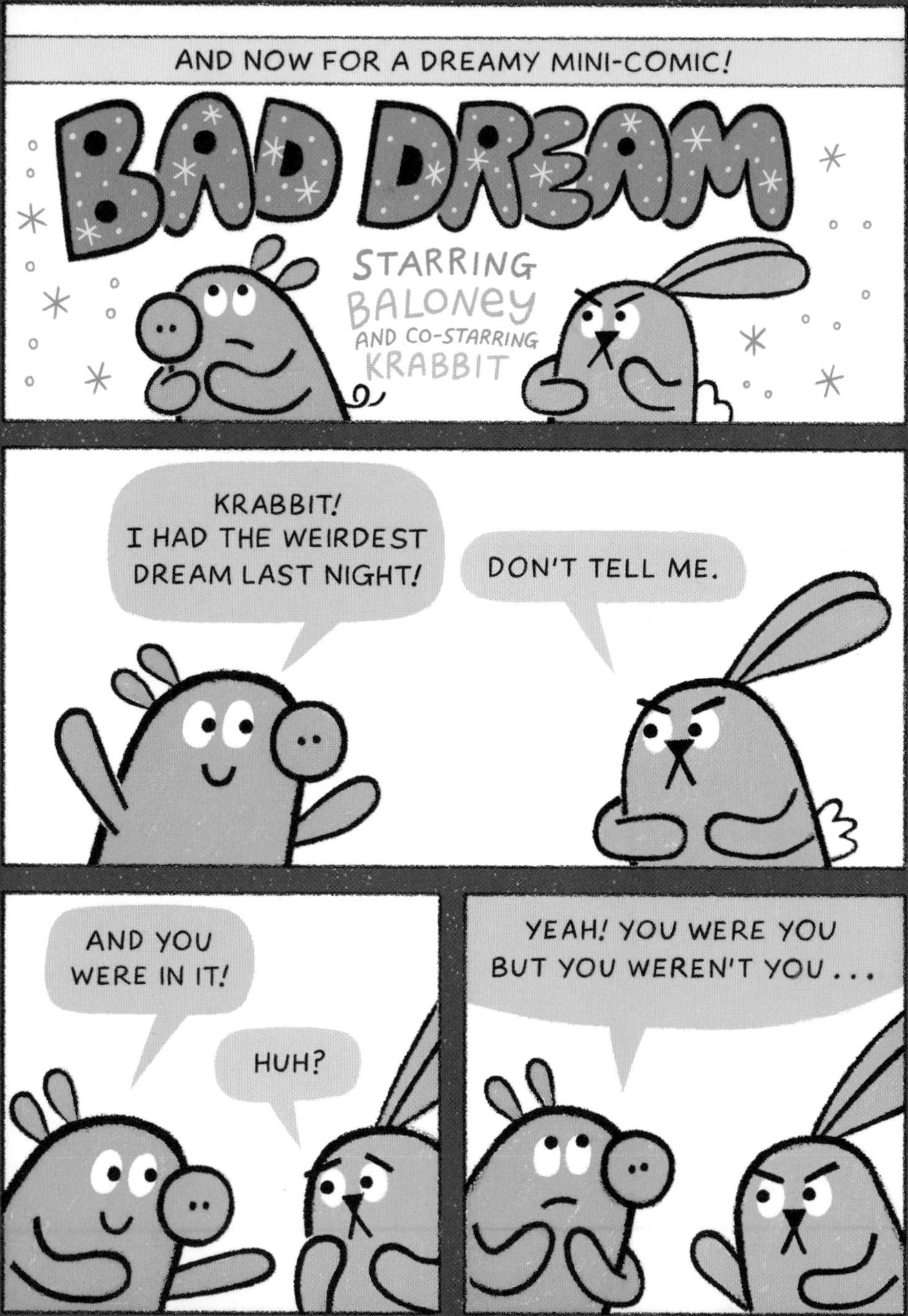
AND NOW FOR A DREAMY MINI-COMIC!
BAD DREAM
STARRING
BALONEY
AND CO-STARRING
KRABBIT
KRABBIT! I HAD THE WEIRDEST DREAM LAST NIGHT!
DON'T TELL ME.
AND YOU WERE IN IT!
HUH?
YEAH! YOU WERE YOU BUT YOU WEREN'T YOU . . .

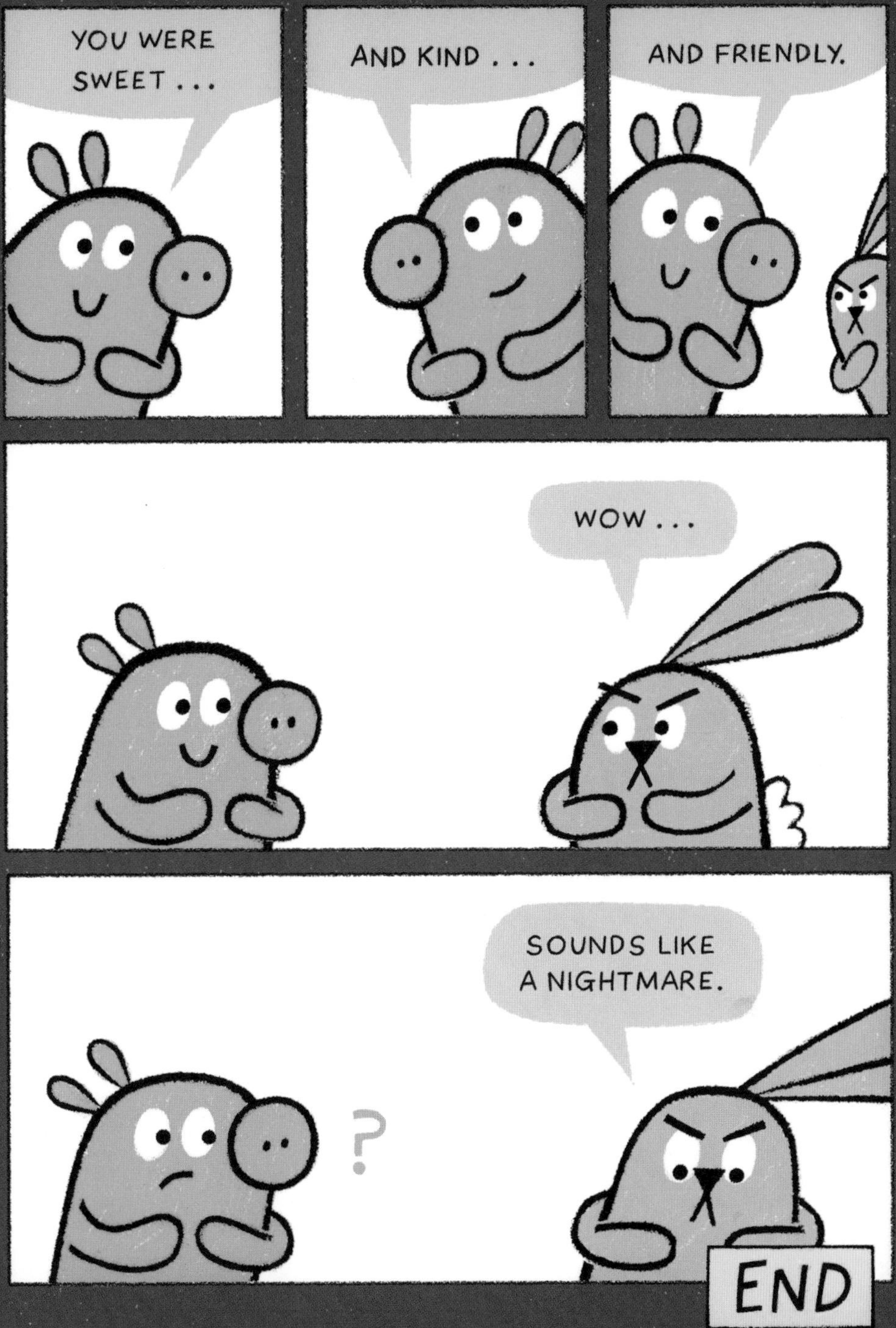

YOU WERE SWEET . . .
AND KIND . . .
AND FRIENDLY.
WOW . . .
SOUNDS LIKE A NIGHTMARE.
?
END

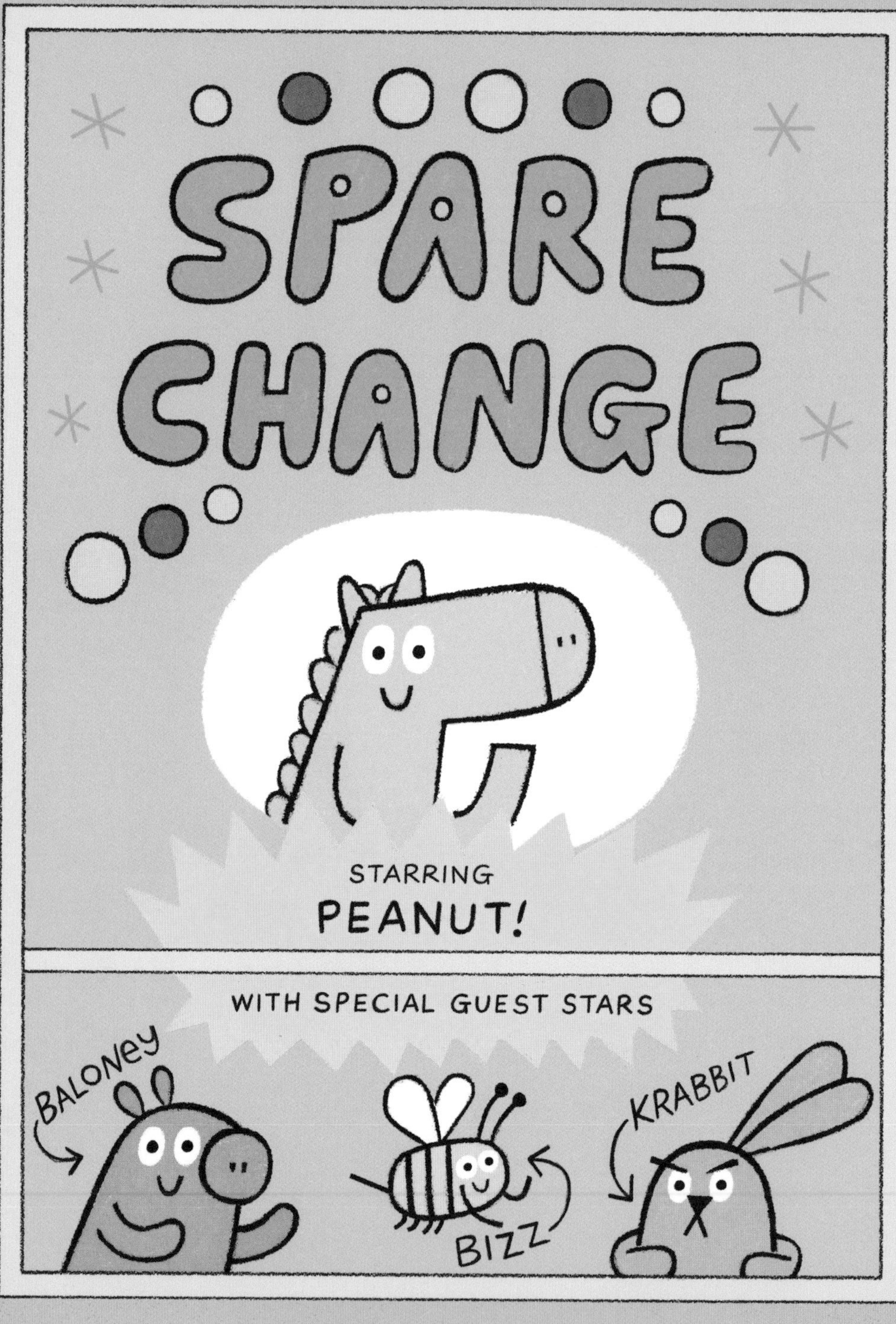
SPARE CHANGE
STARRING
PEANUT!
WITH SPECIAL GUEST STARS
BALONEY
BIZZ
KRABBIT

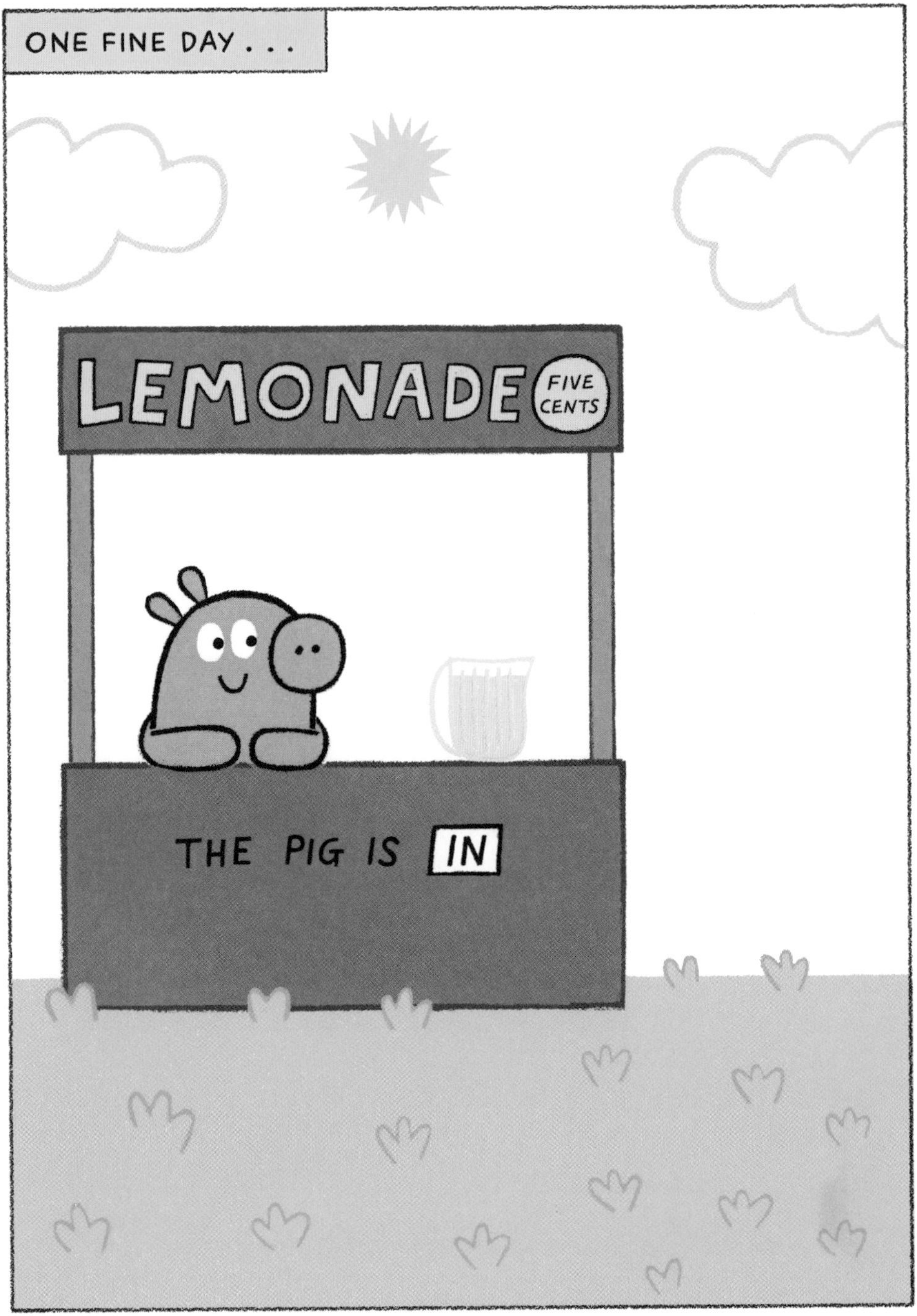
ONE FINE DAY . . .
LEMONADE
FIVE CENTS
THE PIG IS IN

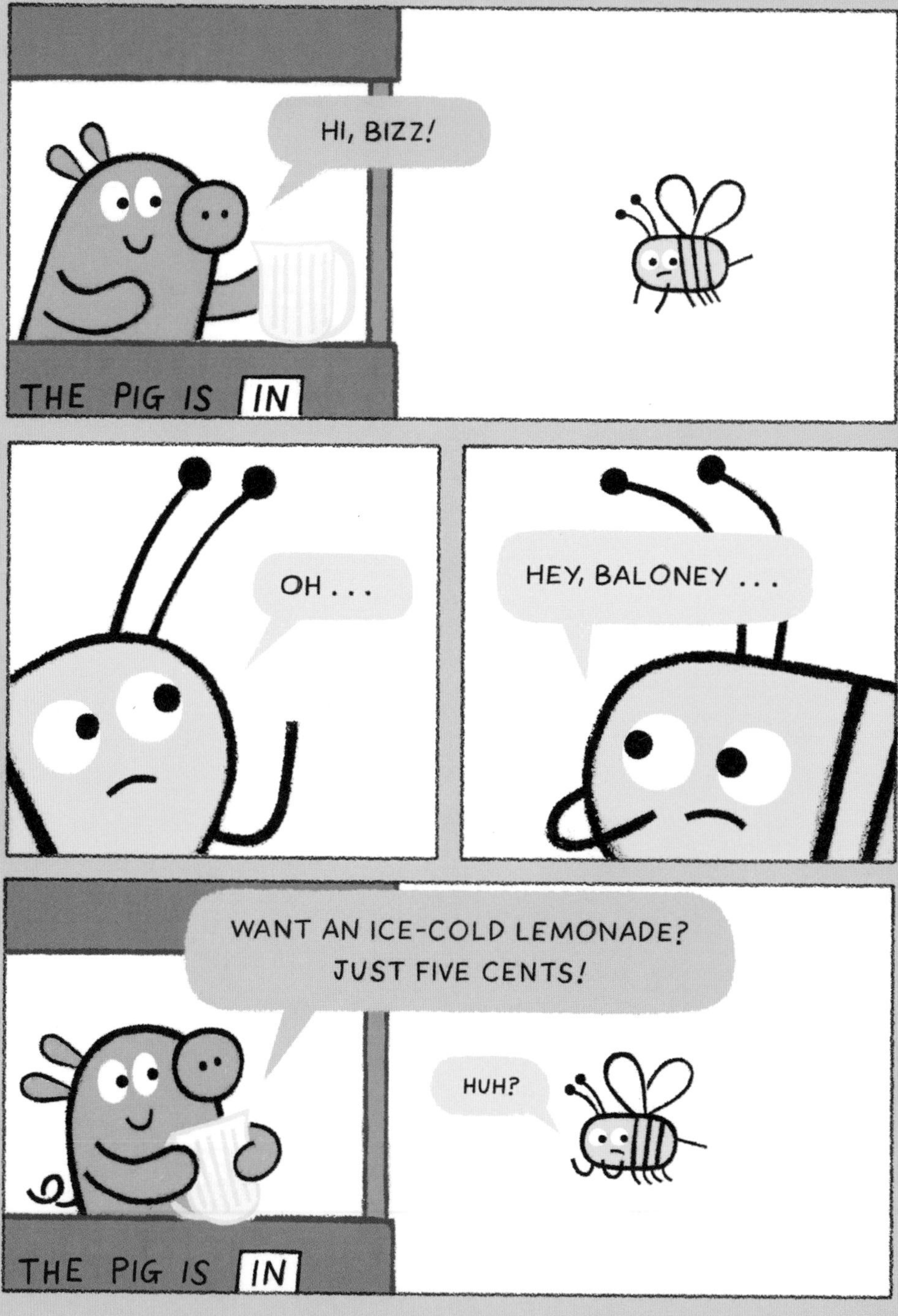
HI, BIZZ!
THE PIG IS IN
OH . . .
HEY, BALONEY . . .
WANT AN ICE-COLD LEMONADE? JUST FIVE CENTS!
HUH?
THE PIG IS IN

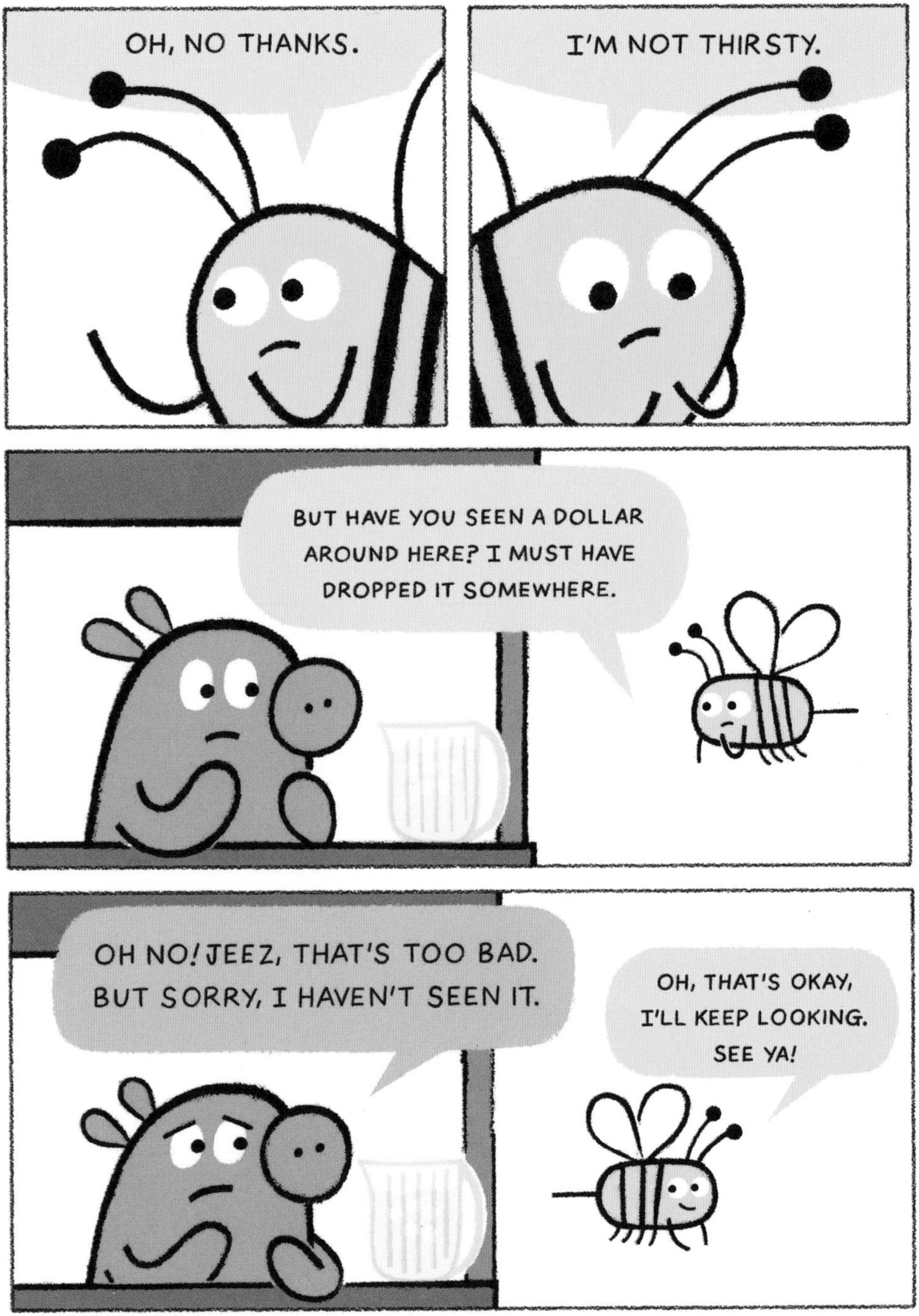
OH, NO THANKS.
I'M NOT THIRSTY.
BUT HAVE YOU SEEN A DOLLAR AROUND HERE? I MUST HAVE DROPPED IT SOMEWHERE.
OH NO! JEEZ, THAT'S TOO BAD. BUT SORRY, I HAVEN'T SEEN IT.
OH, THAT'S OKAY, I'LL KEEP LOOKING. SEE YA!

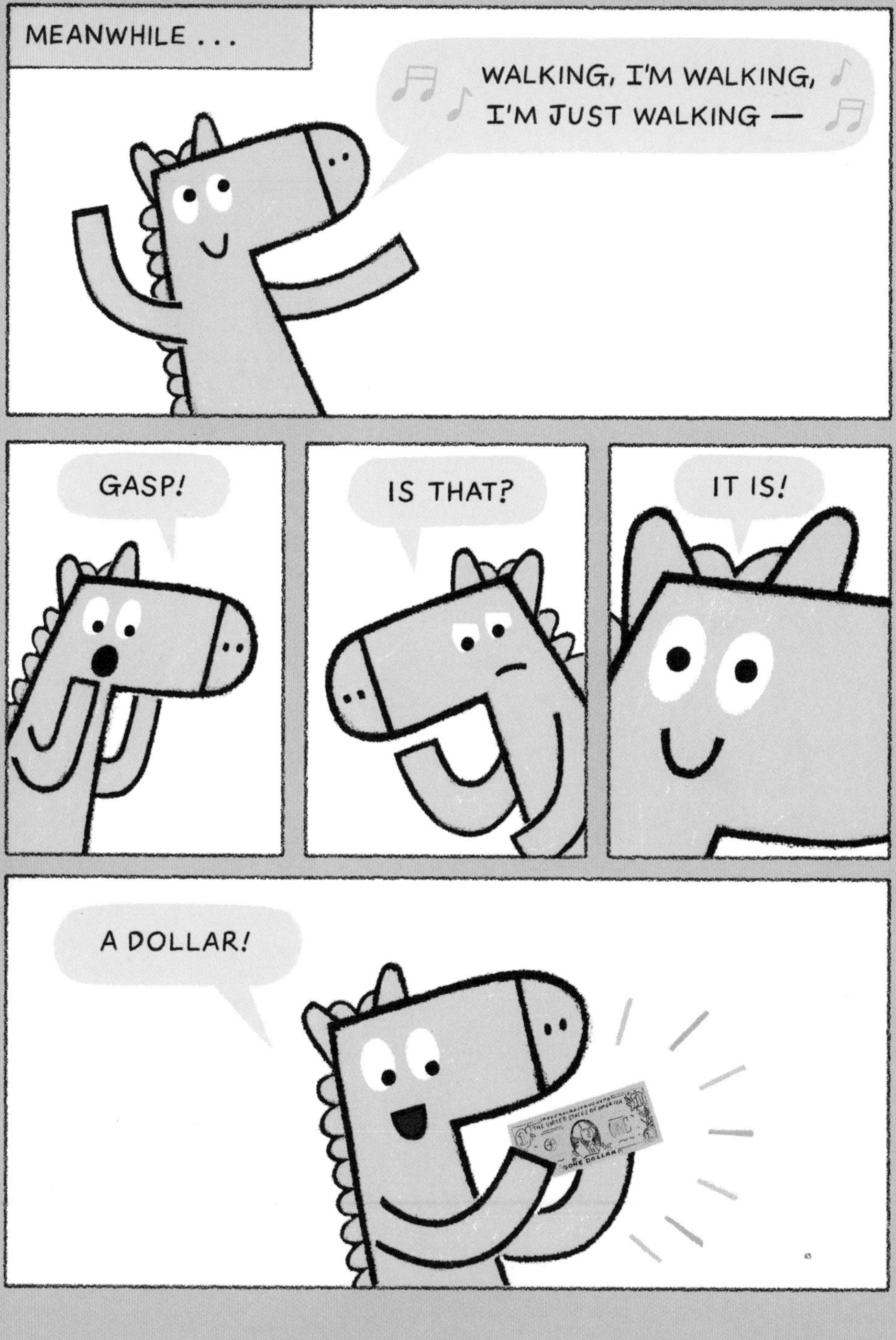
MEANWHILE . . .
WALKING, I'M WALKING, I'M JUST WALKING —
GASP!
IS THAT?
IT IS!
A DOLLAR!

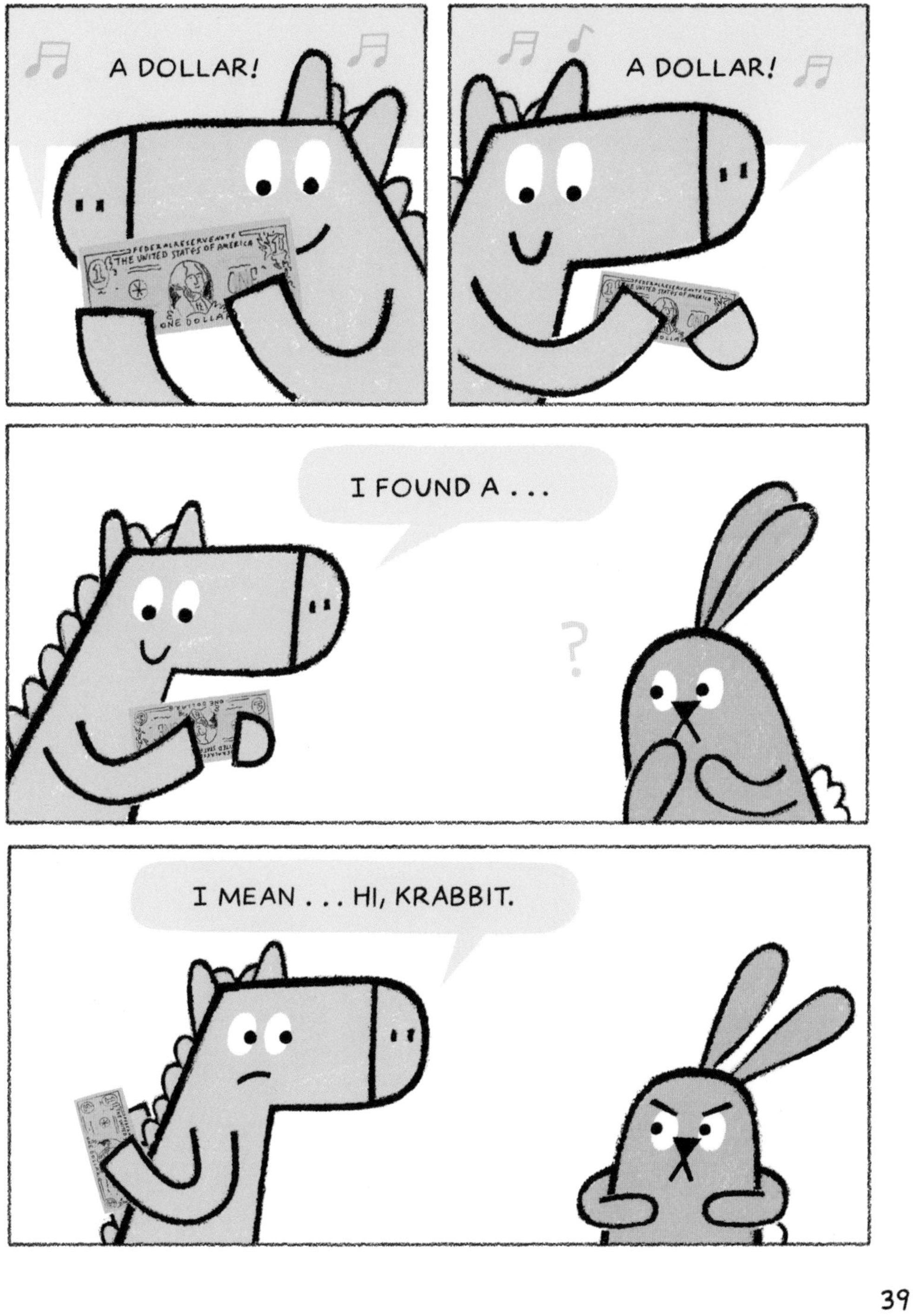
A DOLLAR!
A DOLLAR!
I FOUND A . . .
I MEAN . . . HI, KRABBIT.

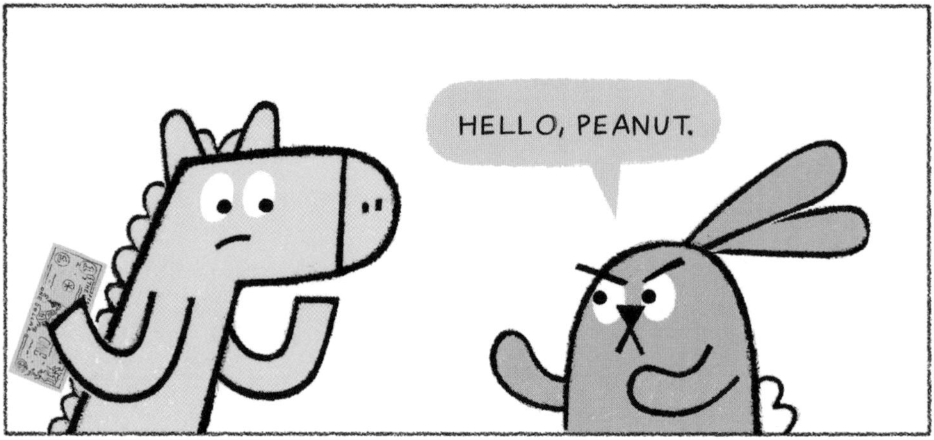
HELLO, PEANUT.

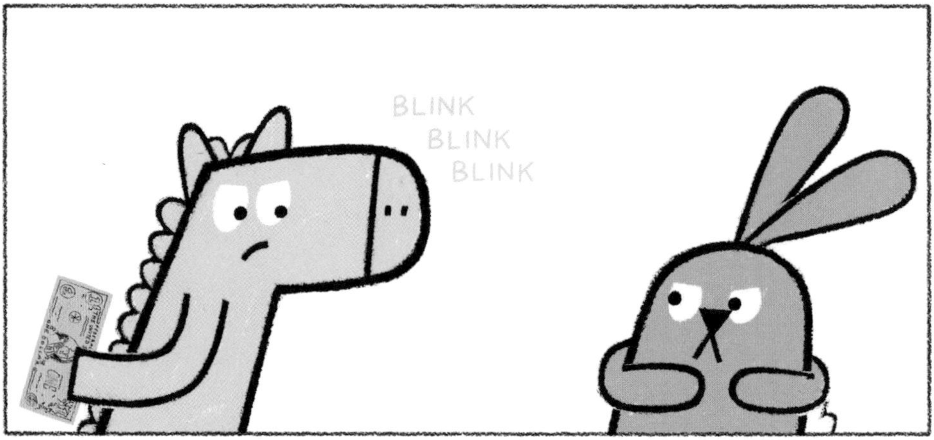
BLINK
BLINK
BLINK

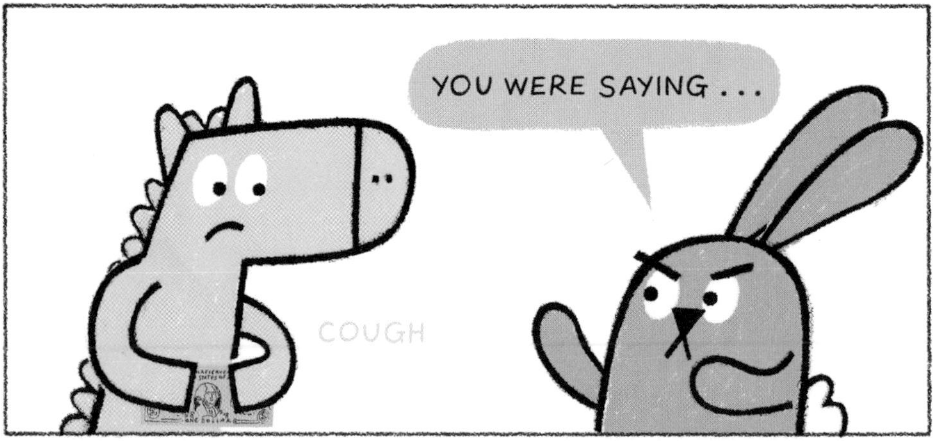
YOU WERE SAYING . . .
COUGH

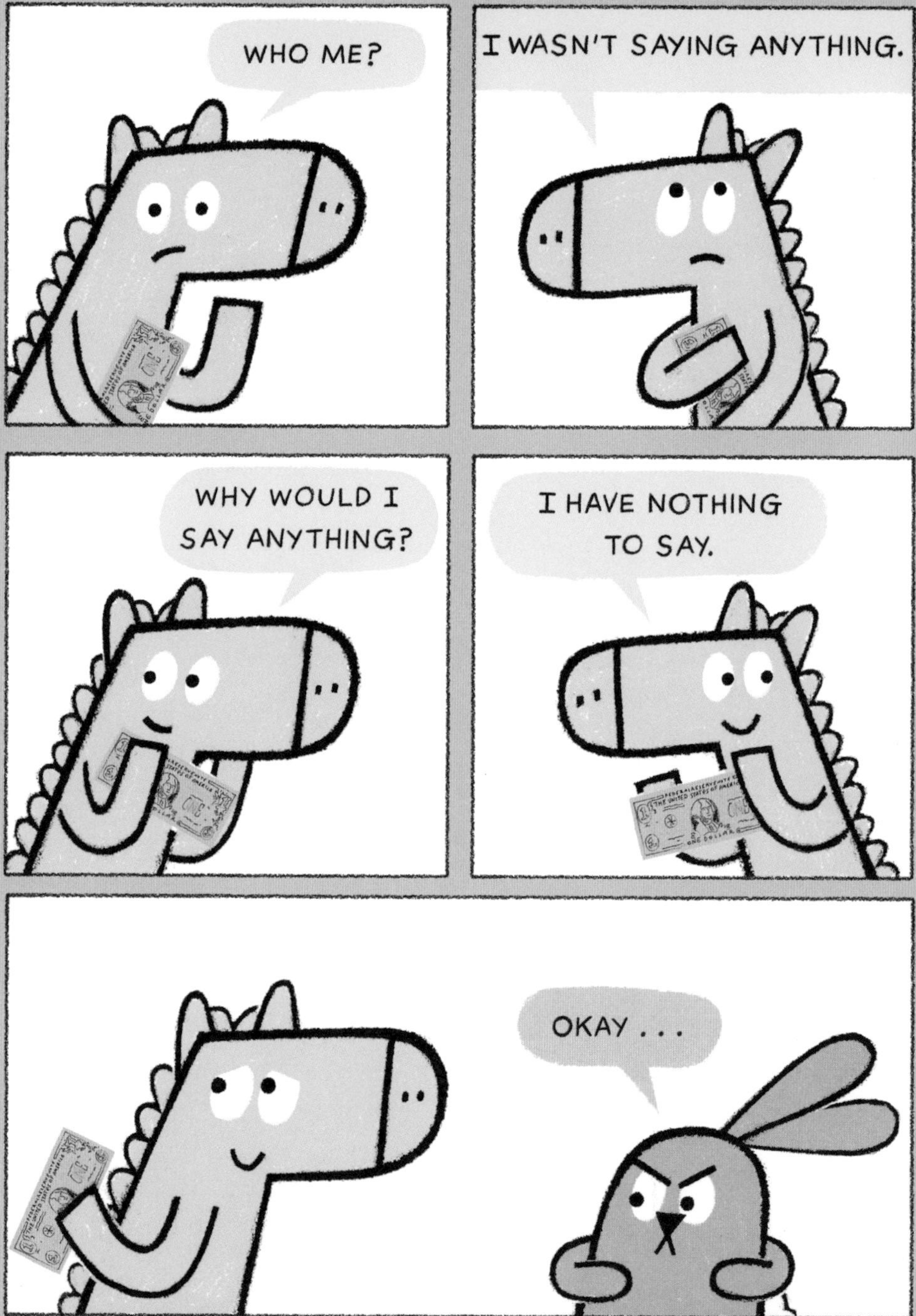
WHO ME?
I WASN'T SAYING ANYTHING.
WHY WOULD I SAY ANYTHING?
I HAVE NOTHING TO SAY.
OKAY . . .

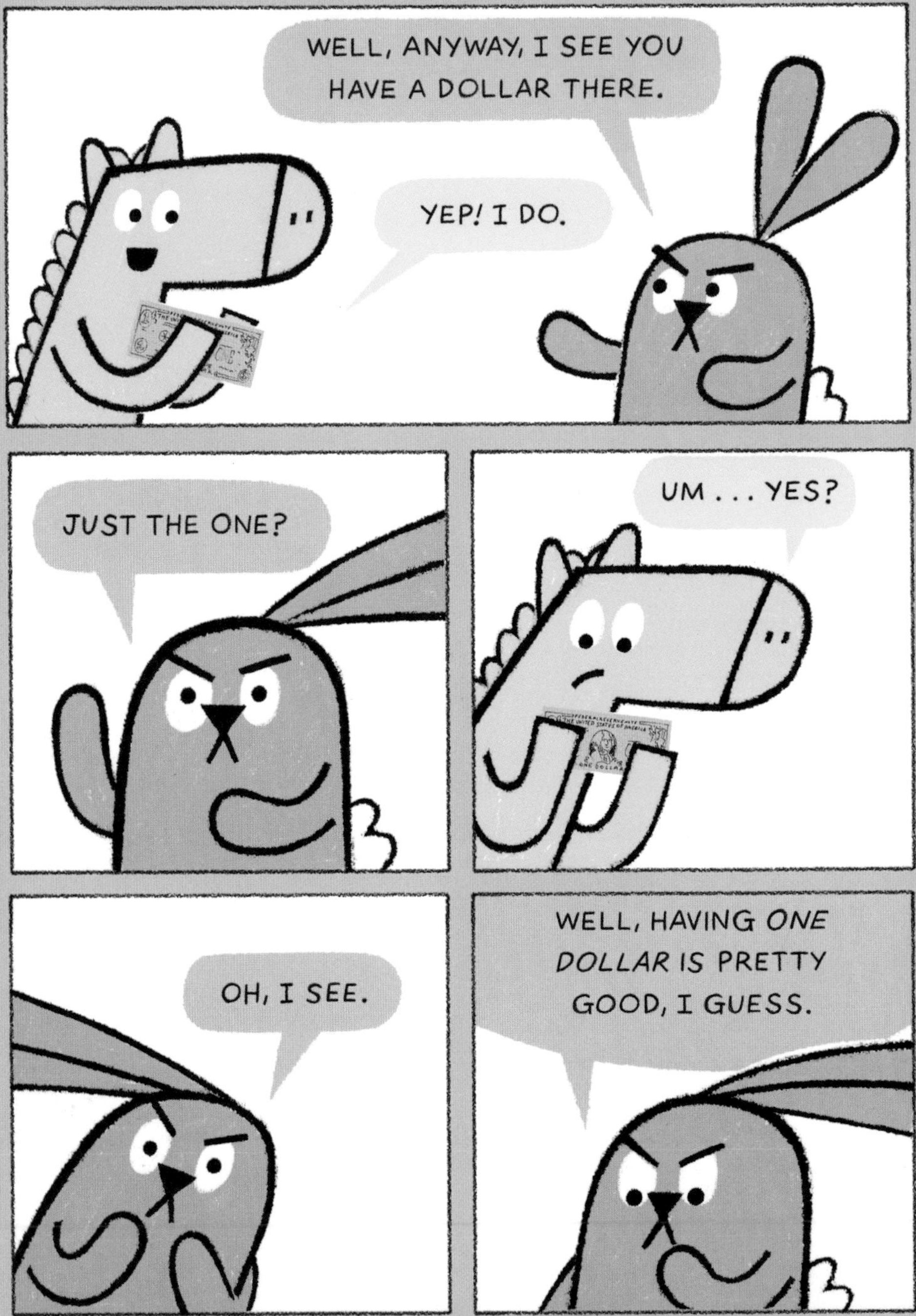
WELL, ANYWAY, I SEE YOU HAVE A DOLLAR THERE.
YEP! I DO.
JUST THE ONE?
UM . . . YES?
OH, I SEE.
WELL, HAVING *ONE DOLLAR* IS PRETTY GOOD, I GUESS.

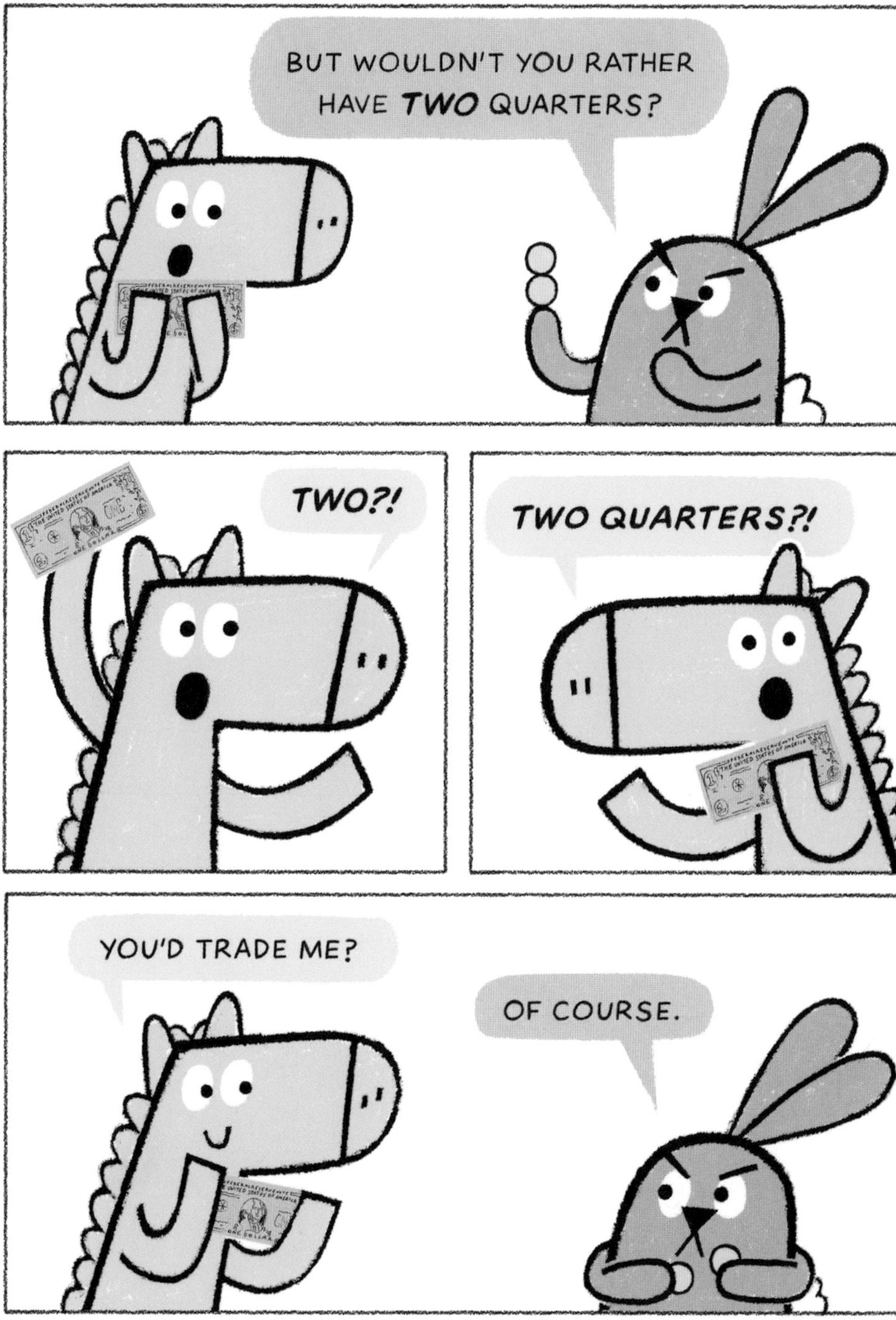
BUT WOULDN'T YOU RATHER HAVE TWO QUARTERS?
TWO?!
TWO QUARTERS?!
YOU'D TRADE ME?
OF COURSE.

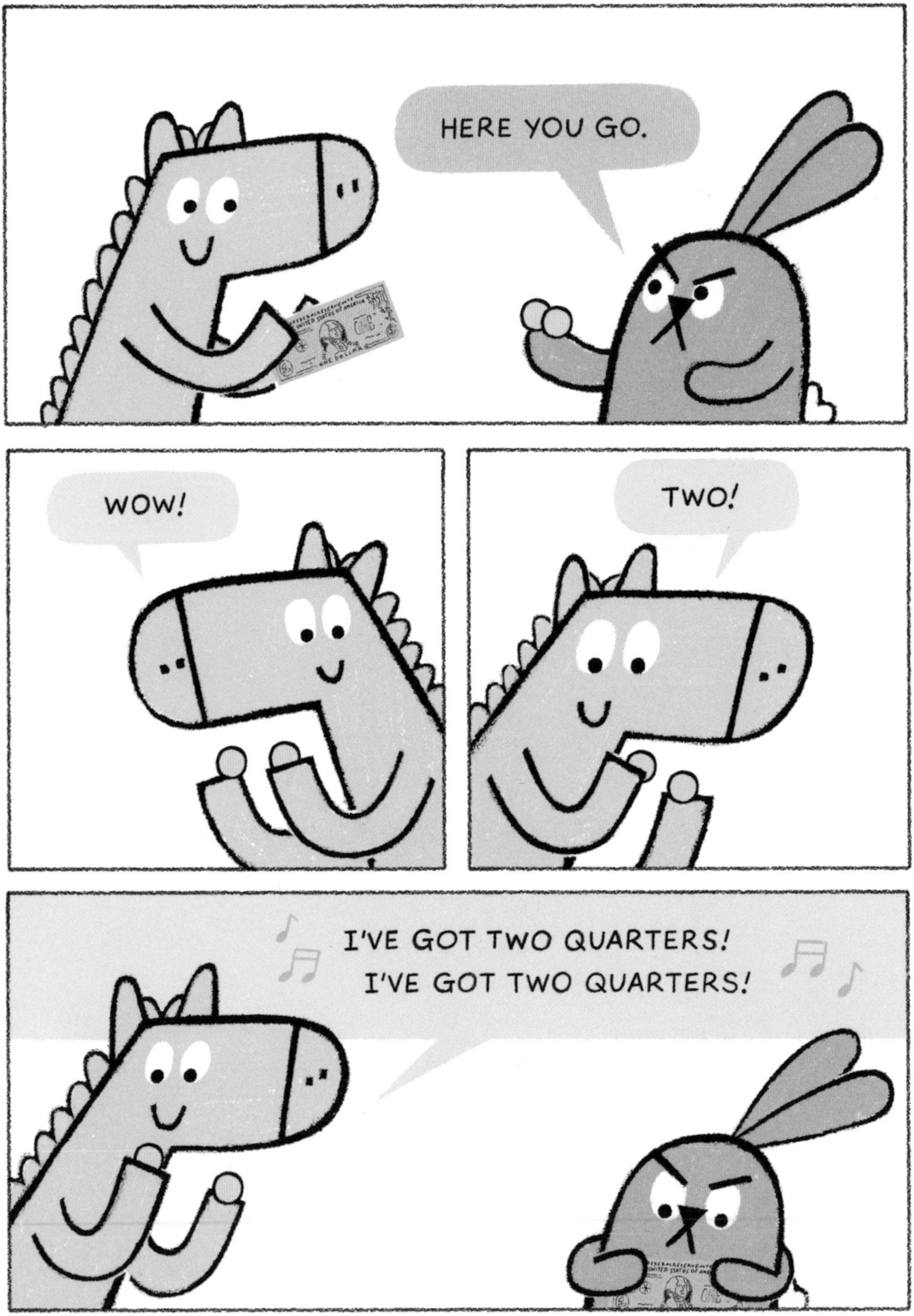
HERE YOU GO.
WOW!
TWO!
I'VE GOT TWO QUARTERS!
I'VE GOT TWO QUARTERS!

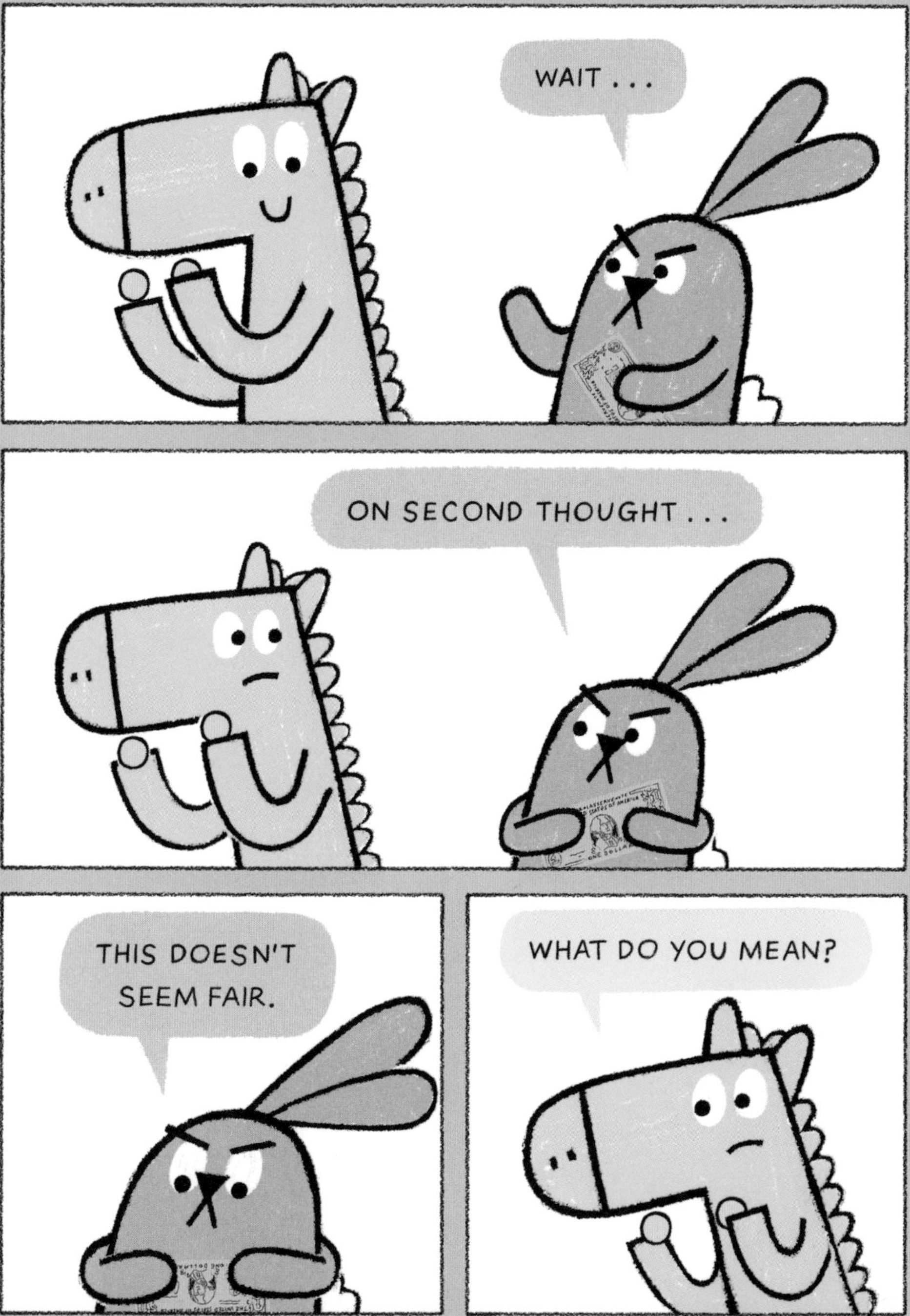
WAIT . . .
ON SECOND THOUGHT . . .
THIS DOESN'T SEEM FAIR.
WHAT DO YOU MEAN?

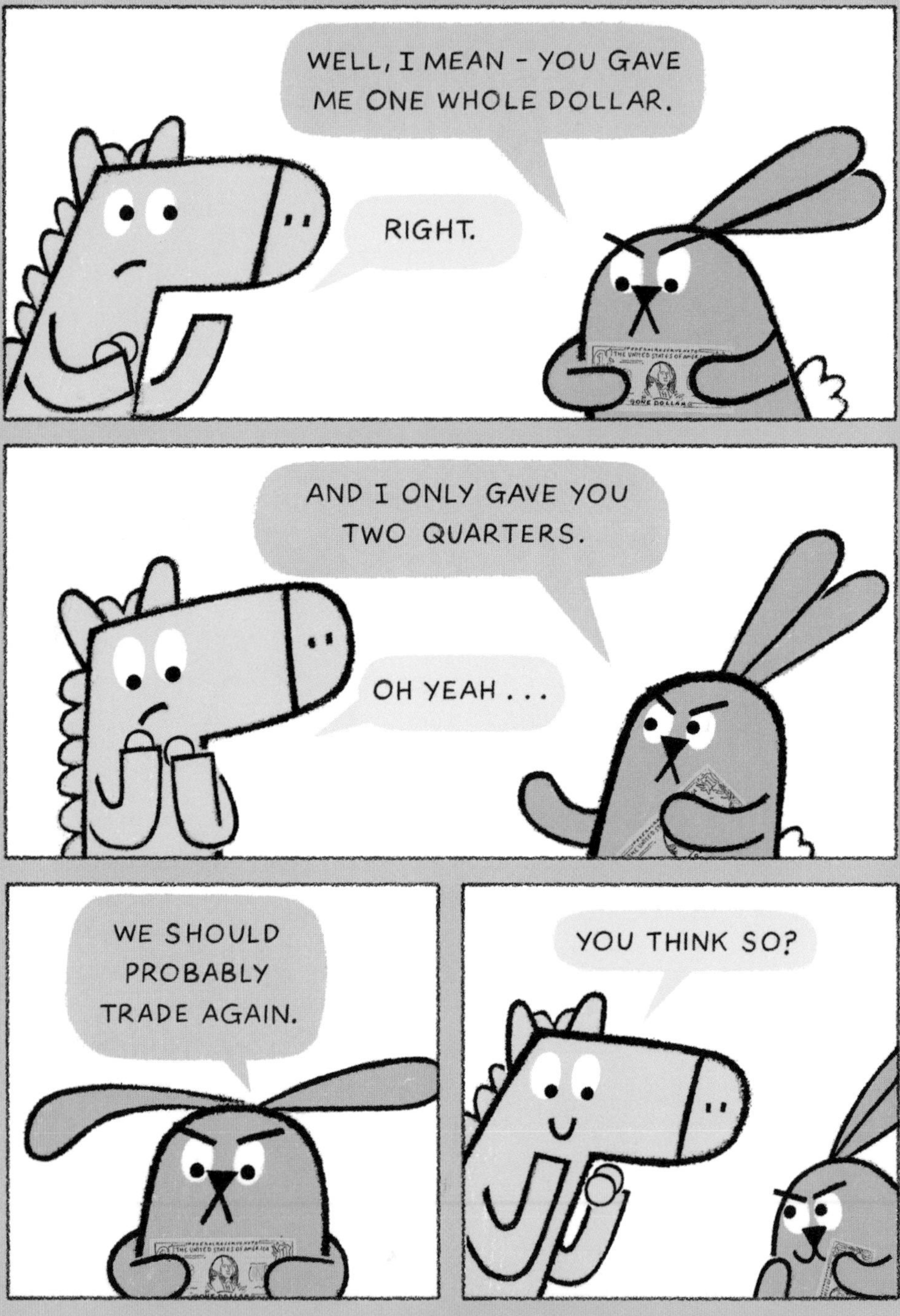
WELL, I MEAN - YOU GAVE ME ONE WHOLE DOLLAR.
RIGHT.
AND I ONLY GAVE YOU TWO QUARTERS.
OH YEAH . . .
WE SHOULD PROBABLY TRADE AGAIN.
YOU THINK SO?

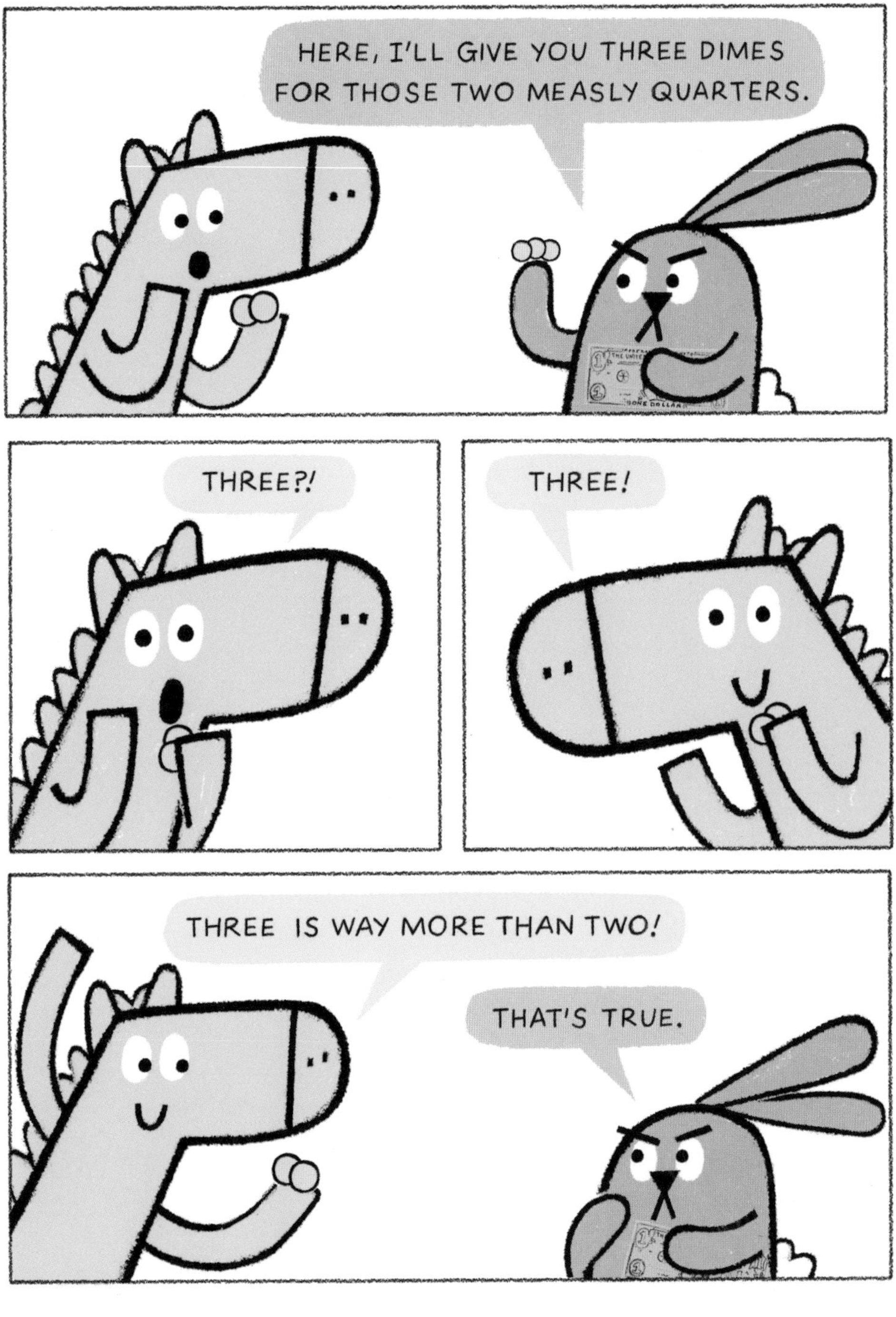
HERE, I'LL GIVE YOU THREE DIMES FOR THOSE TWO MEASLY QUARTERS.
THREE?!
THREE!
THREE IS WAY MORE THAN TWO!
THAT'S TRUE.

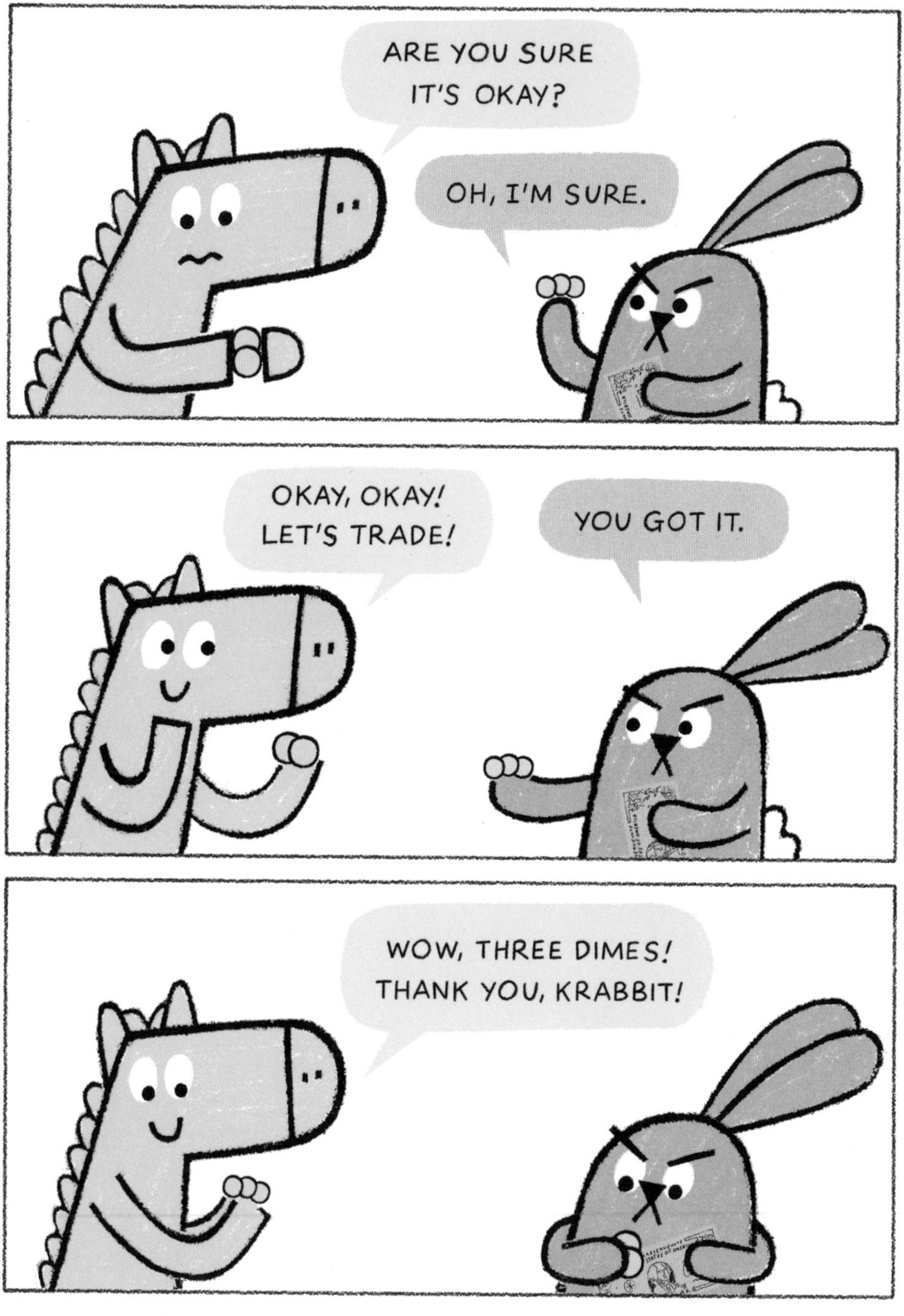
ARE YOU SURE IT'S OKAY?
OH, I'M SURE.
OKAY, OKAY! LET'S TRADE!
YOU GOT IT.
WOW, THREE DIMES! THANK YOU, KRABBIT!

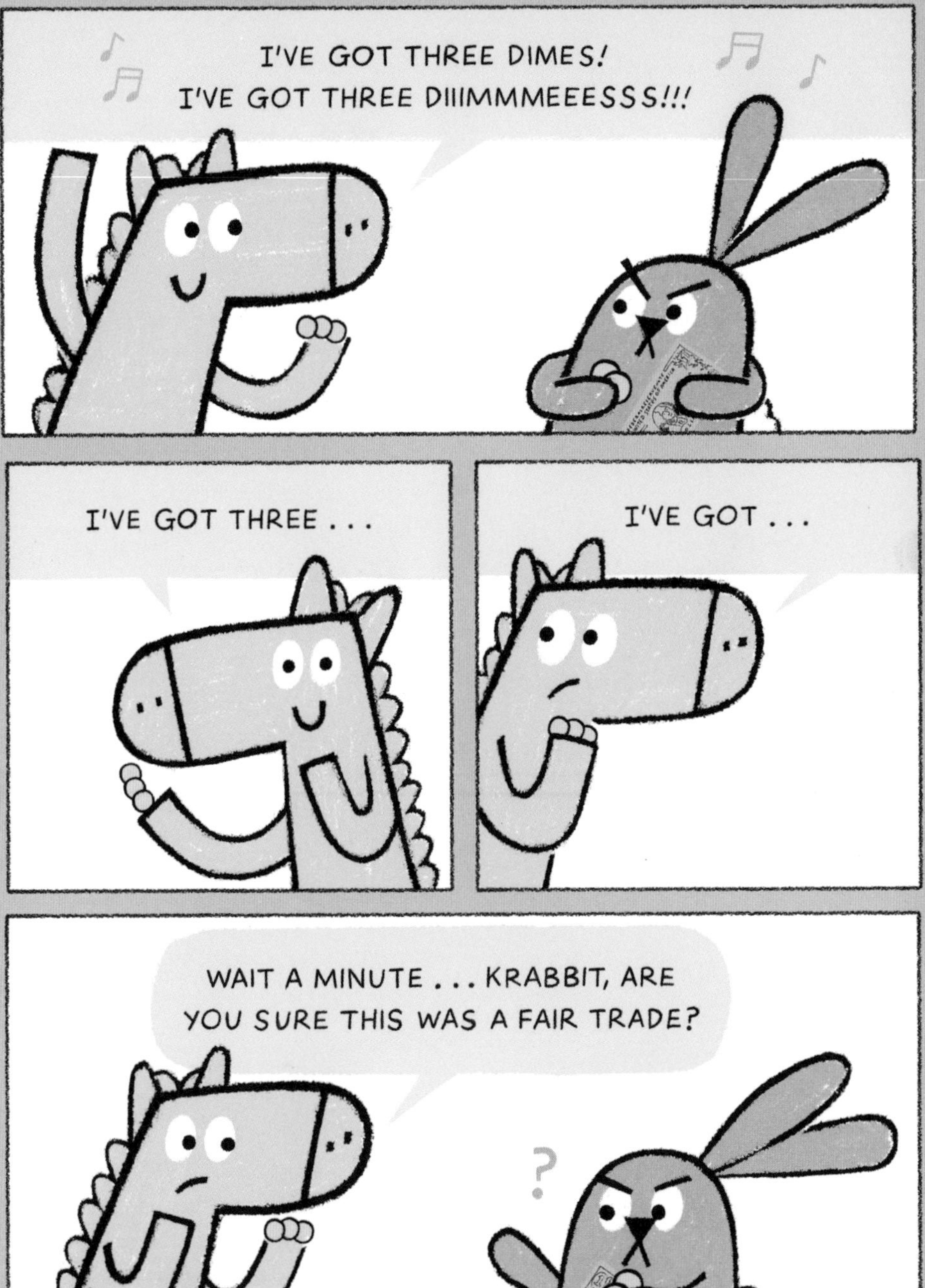
I'VE GOT THREE DIMES!
I'VE GOT THREE DIIIMMMEEESSS!!!
I'VE GOT THREE . . .
I'VE GOT . . .
WAIT A MINUTE . . . KRABBIT, ARE YOU SURE THIS WAS A FAIR TRADE?
?

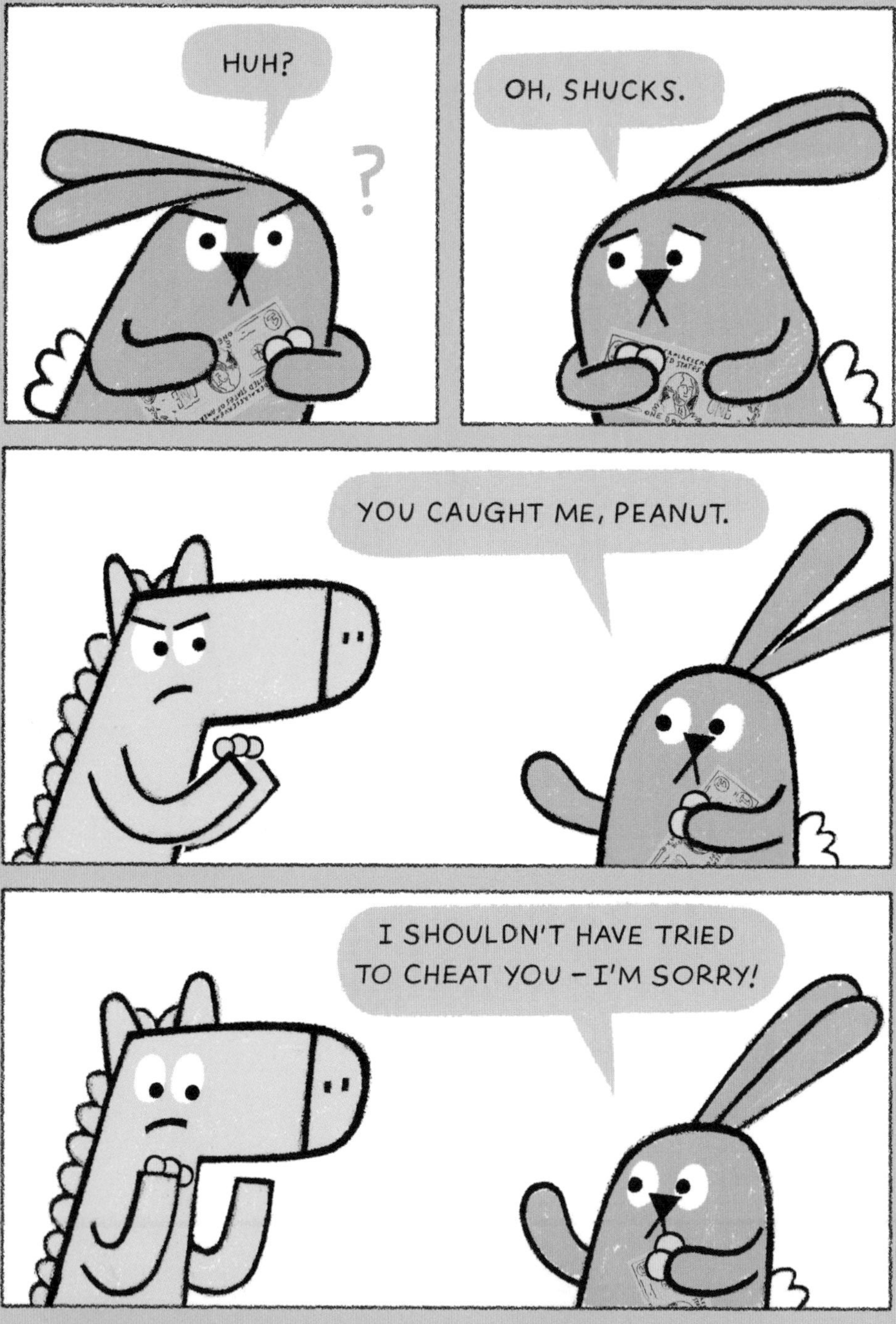
HUH?
OH, SHUCKS.
YOU CAUGHT ME, PEANUT.
I SHOULDN'T HAVE TRIED TO CHEAT YOU – I'M SORRY!

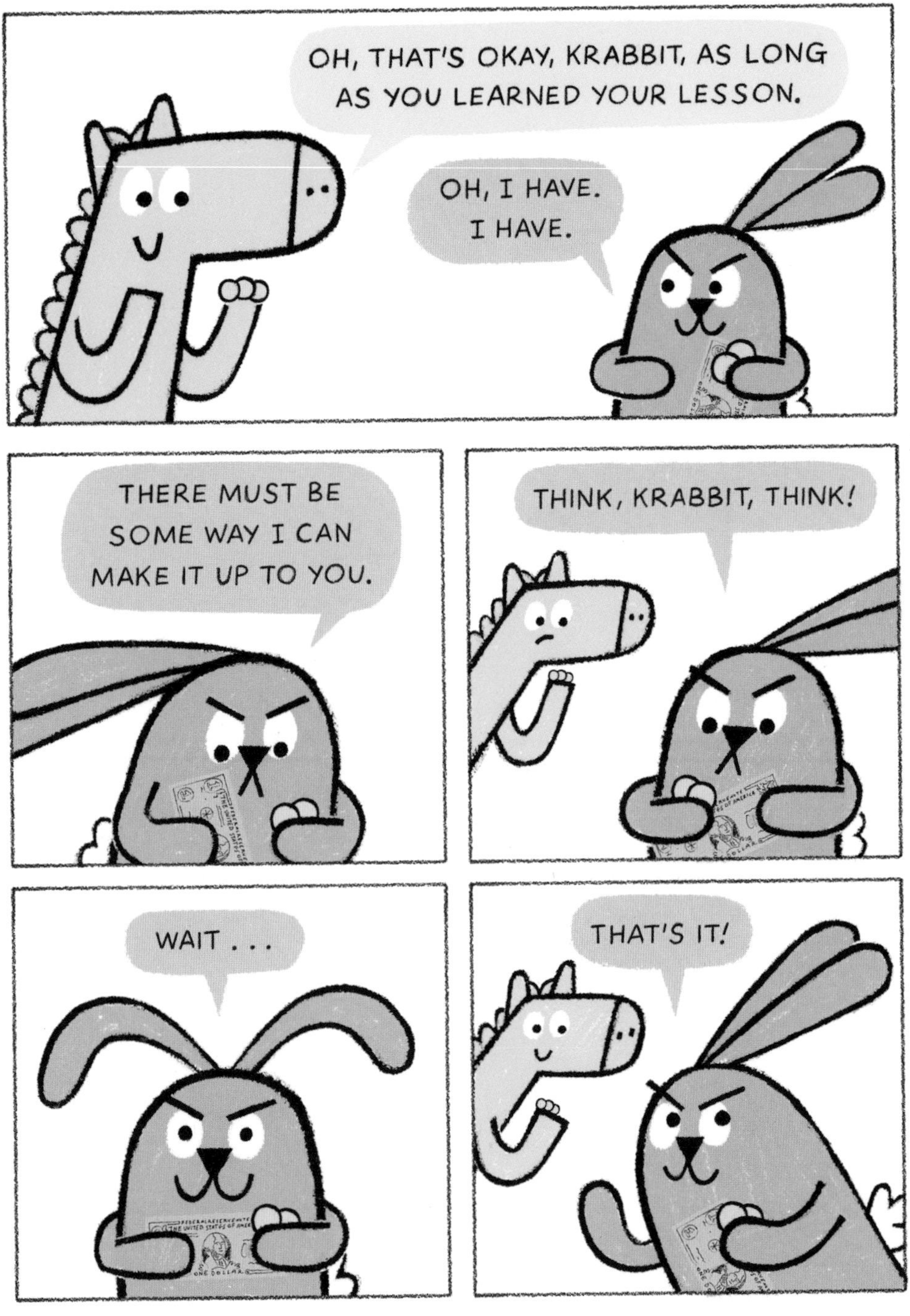
OH, THAT'S OKAY, KRABBIT, AS LONG AS YOU LEARNED YOUR LESSON.
OH, I HAVE. I HAVE.
THERE MUST BE SOME WAY I CAN MAKE IT UP TO YOU.
THINK, KRABBIT, THINK!
WAIT . . .
THAT'S IT!

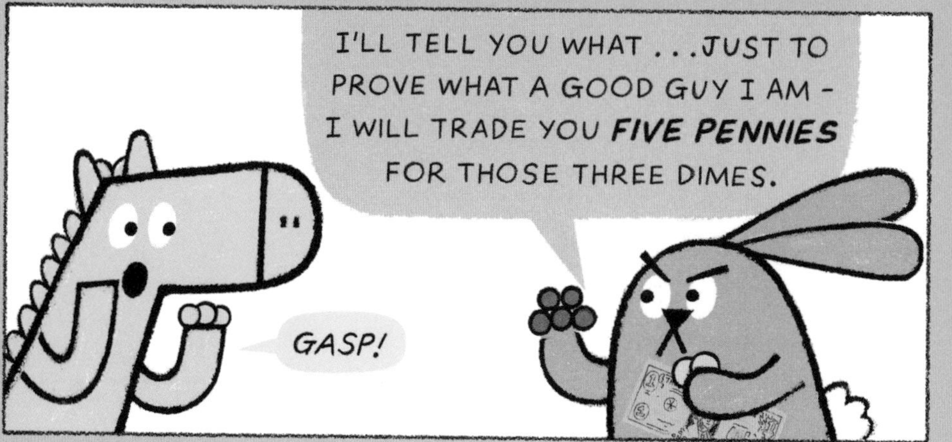
I'LL TELL YOU WHAT . . . JUST TO PROVE WHAT A GOOD GUY I AM - I WILL TRADE YOU ***FIVE PENNIES*** FOR THOSE THREE DIMES.
GASP!

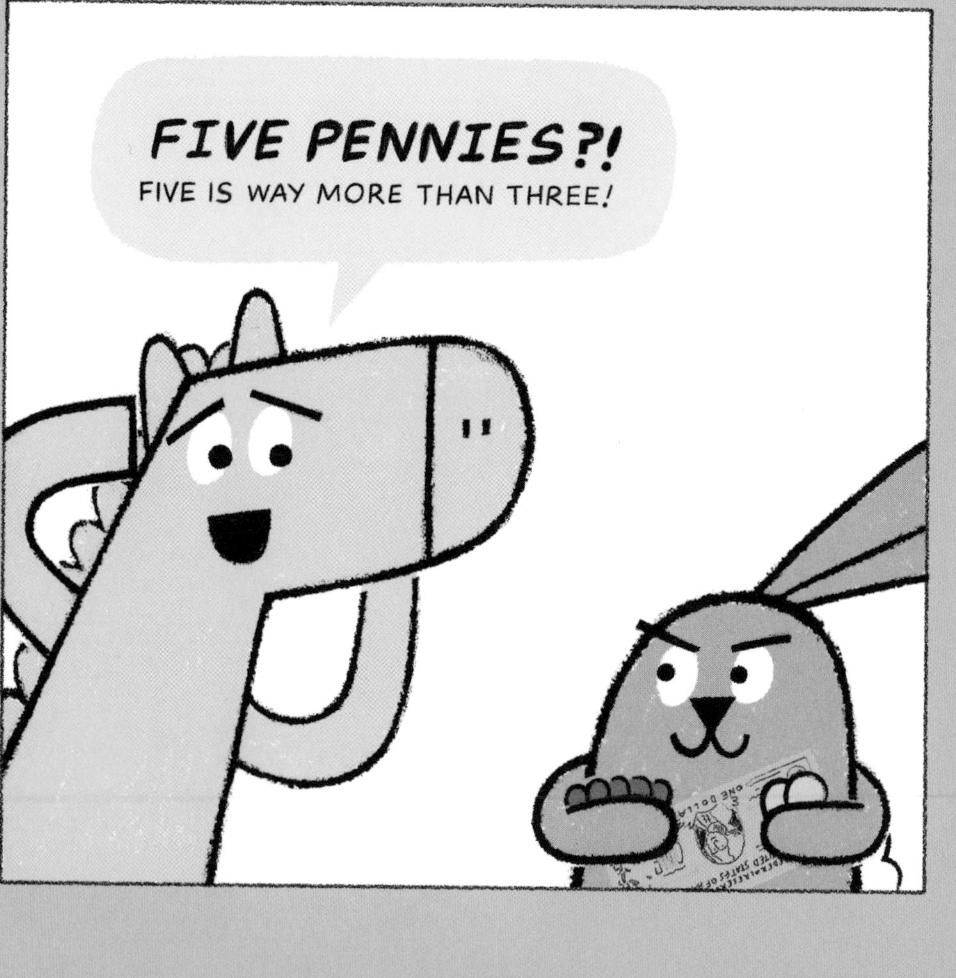
FIVE PENNIES?!
FIVE IS WAY MORE THAN THREE!

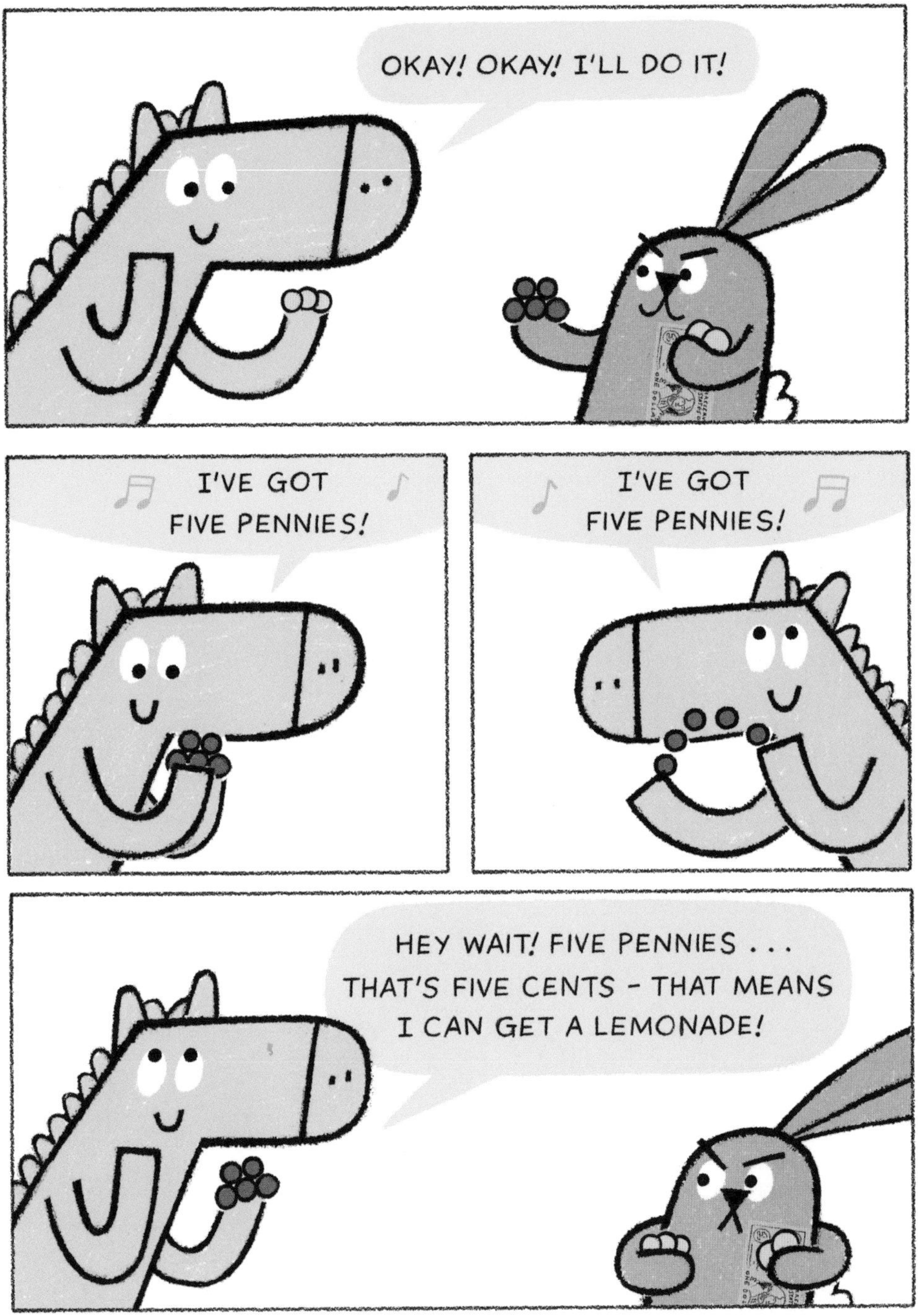
OKAY! OKAY! I'LL DO IT!
I'VE GOT FIVE PENNIES!
I'VE GOT FIVE PENNIES!
HEY WAIT! FIVE PENNIES . . . THAT'S FIVE CENTS - THAT MEANS I CAN GET A LEMONADE!

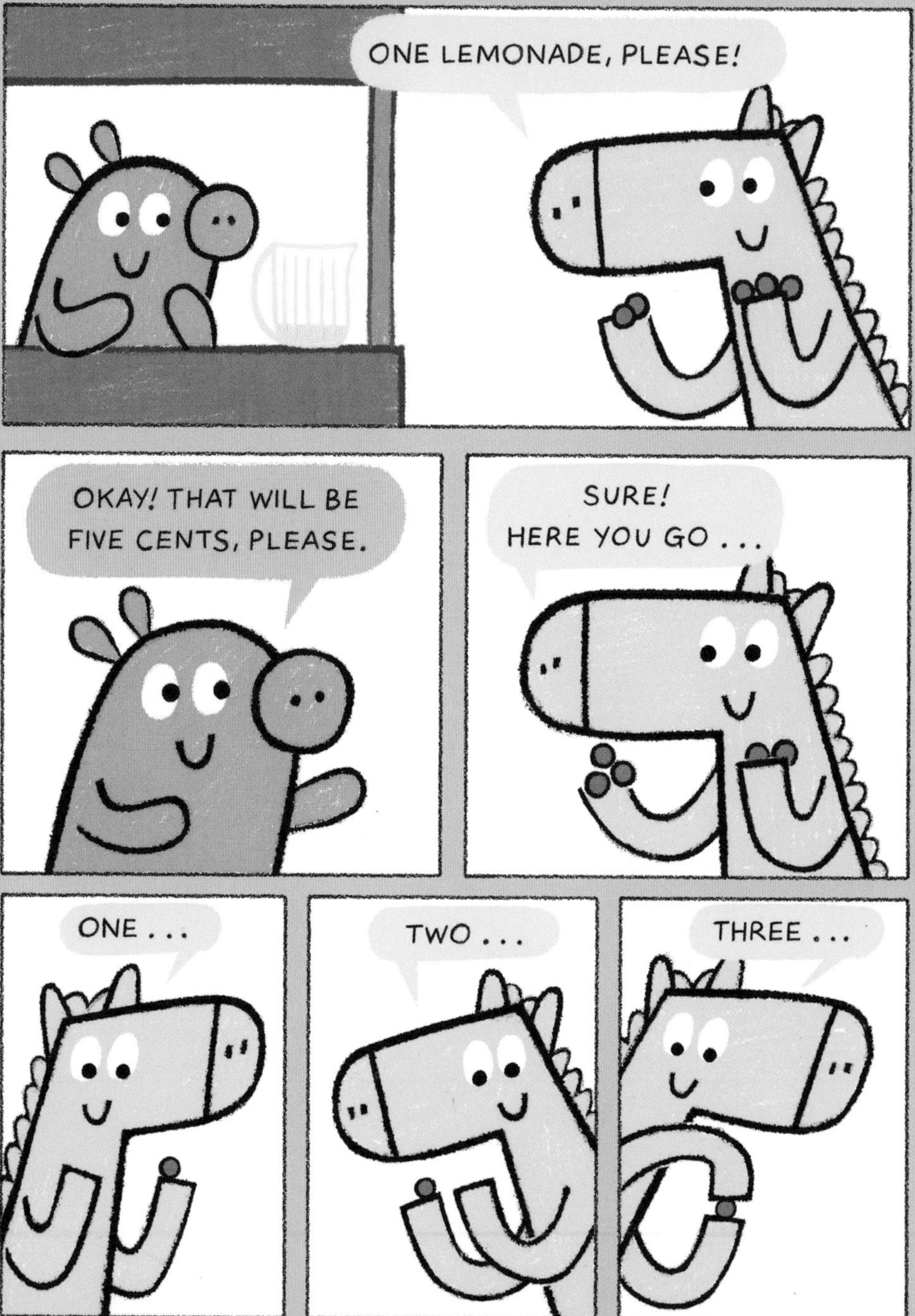

ONE LEMONADE, PLEASE!
OKAY! THAT WILL BE FIVE CENTS, PLEASE.
SURE! HERE YOU GO . . .
ONE . . .
TWO . . .
THREE . . .

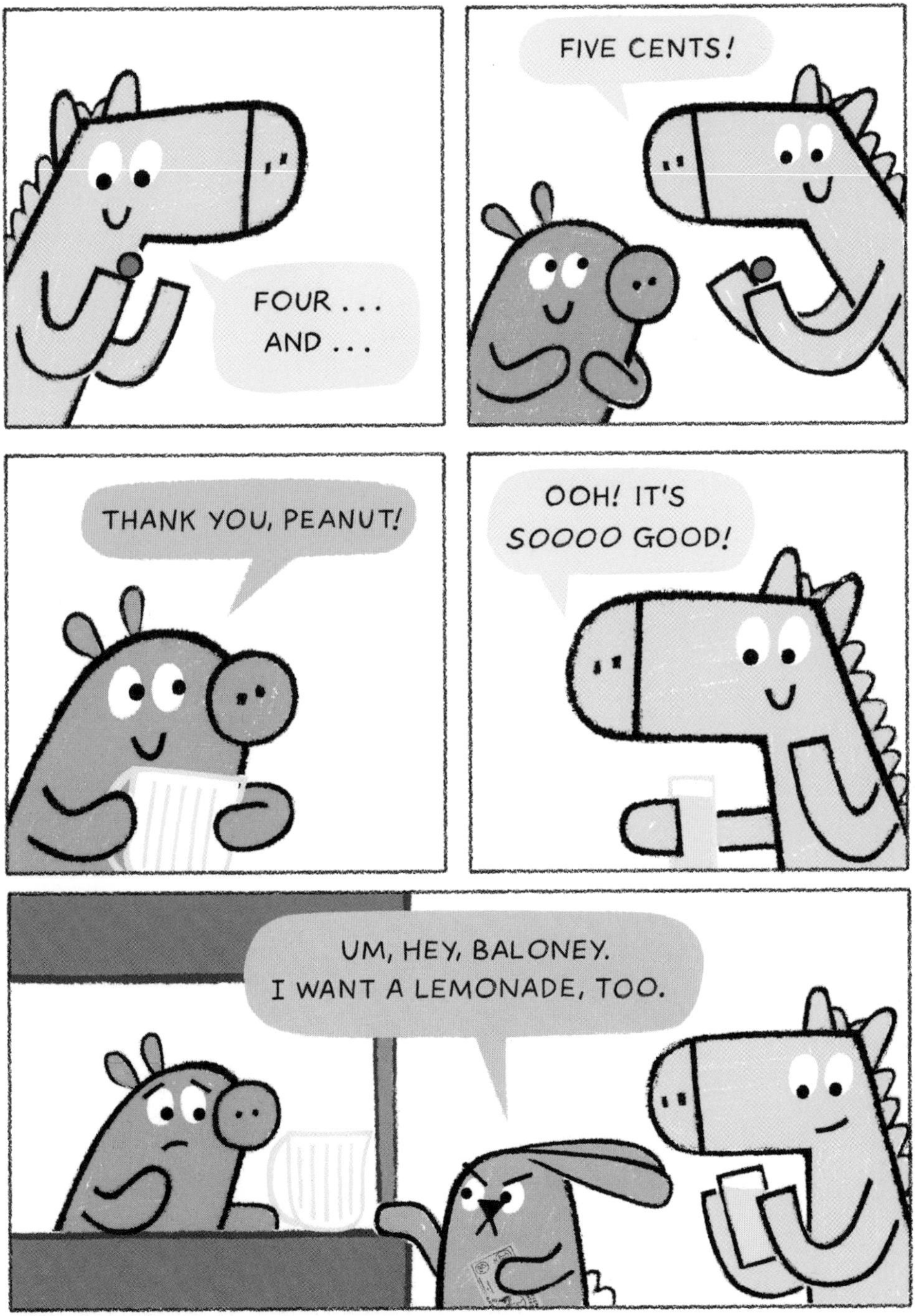
FOUR . . .
AND . . .
FIVE CENTS!
THANK YOU, PEANUT!
OOH! IT'S
SOOOO GOOD!
UM, HEY, BALONEY.
I WANT A LEMONADE, TOO.

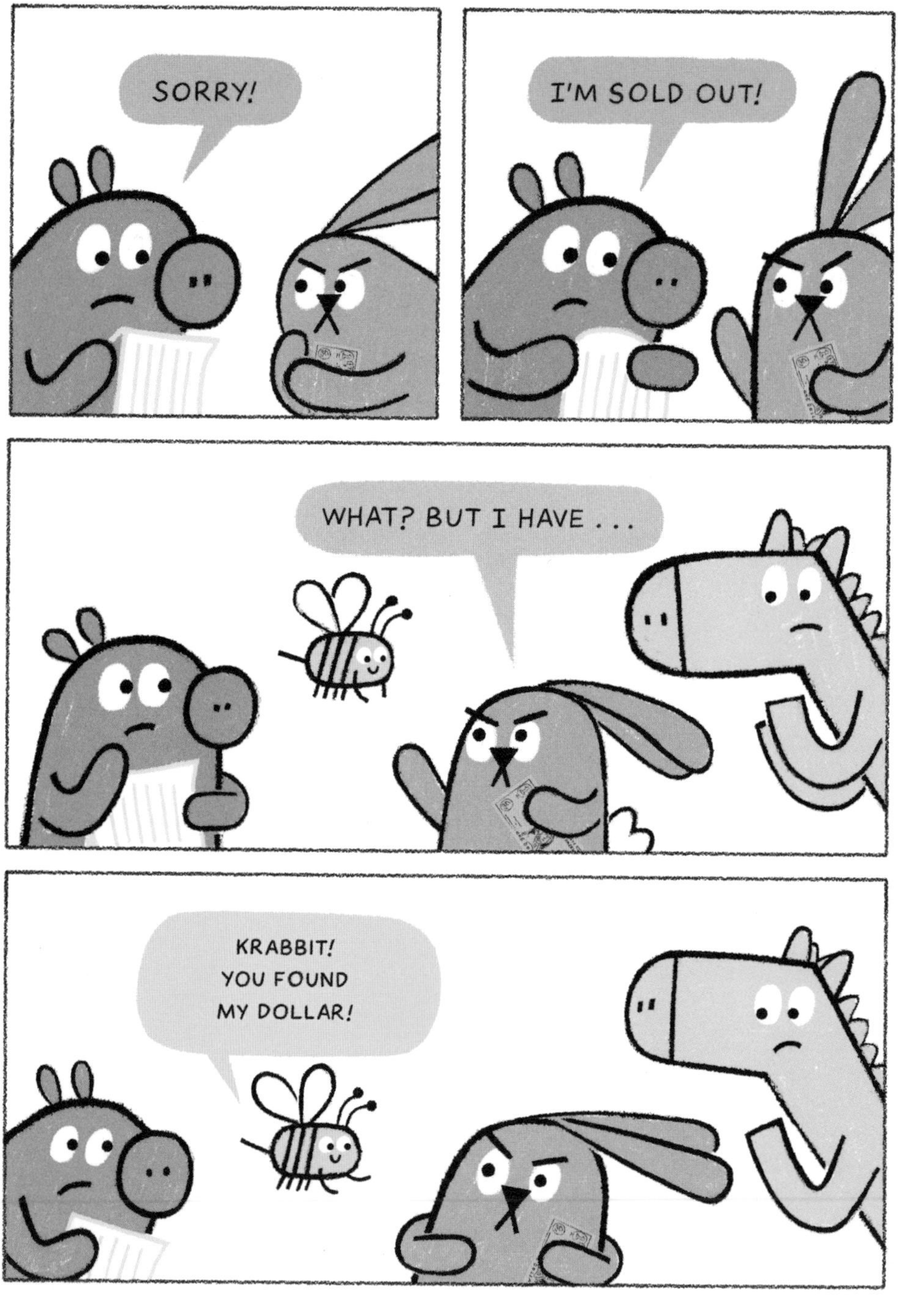
SORRY!
I'M SOLD OUT!
WHAT? BUT I HAVE . . .
KRABBIT! YOU FOUND MY DOLLAR!

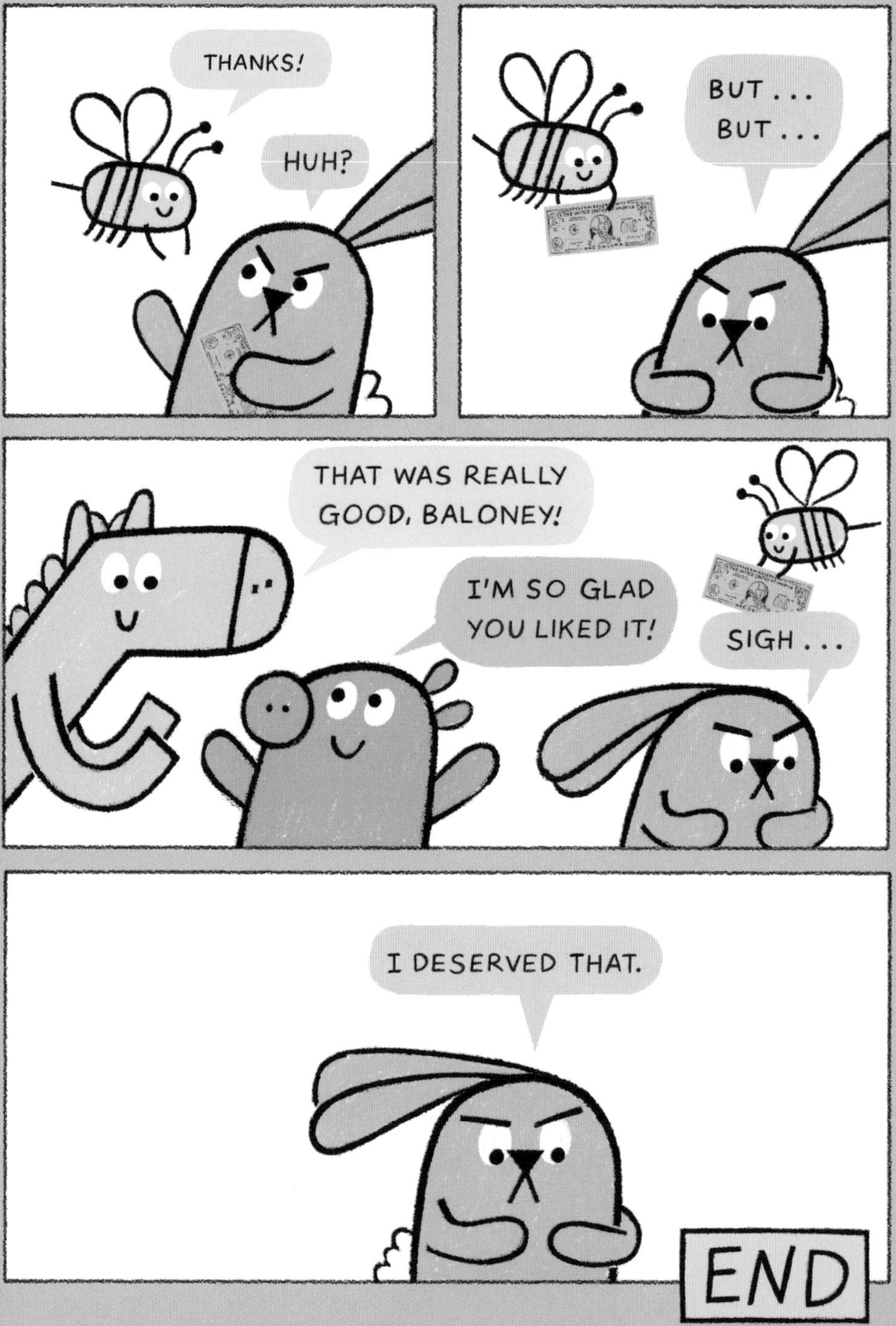
THANKS!
HUH?
BUT . . .
BUT . . .
THAT WAS REALLY GOOD, BALONEY!
I'M SO GLAD YOU LIKED IT!
SIGH . . .
I DESERVED THAT.
END

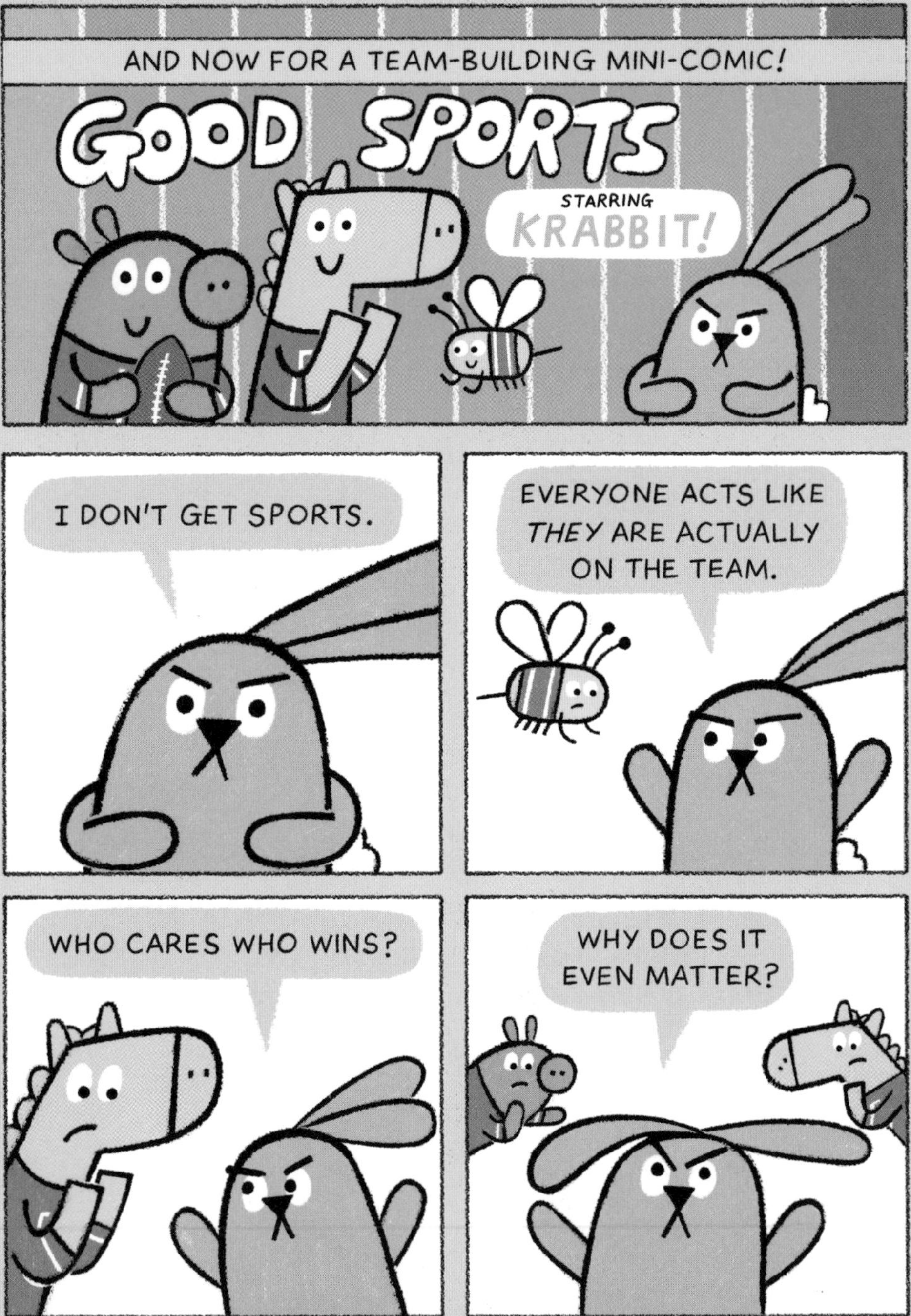
AND NOW FOR A TEAM-BUILDING MINI-COMIC!
GOOD SPORTS
STARRING KRABBIT!
I DON'T GET SPORTS.
EVERYONE ACTS LIKE *THEY* ARE ACTUALLY ON THE TEAM.
WHO CARES WHO WINS?
WHY DOES IT EVEN MATTER?

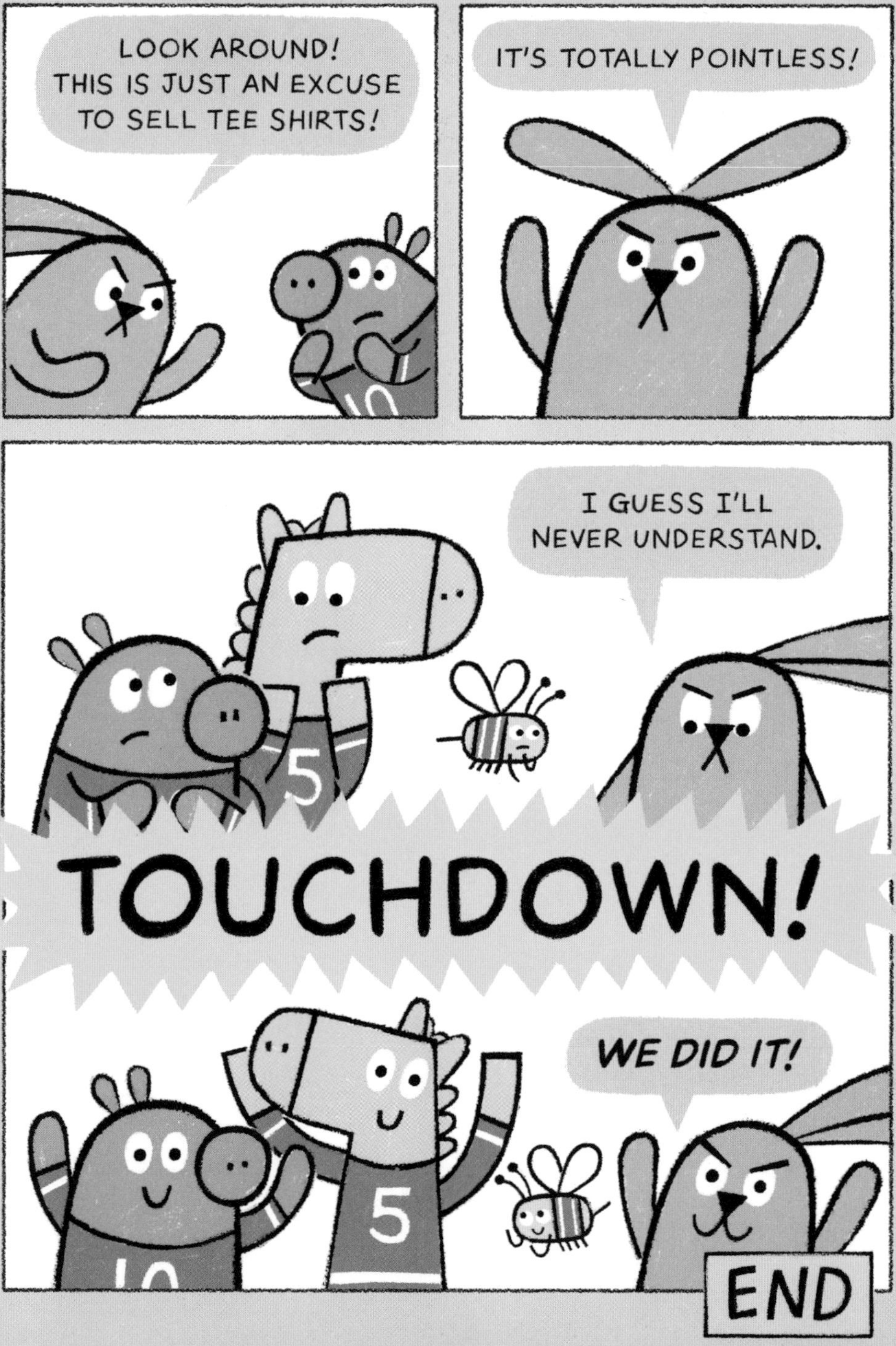
LOOK AROUND! THIS IS JUST AN EXCUSE TO SELL TEE SHIRTS!
IT'S TOTALLY POINTLESS!
I GUESS I'LL NEVER UNDERSTAND.
TOUCHDOWN!
WE DID IT!
END

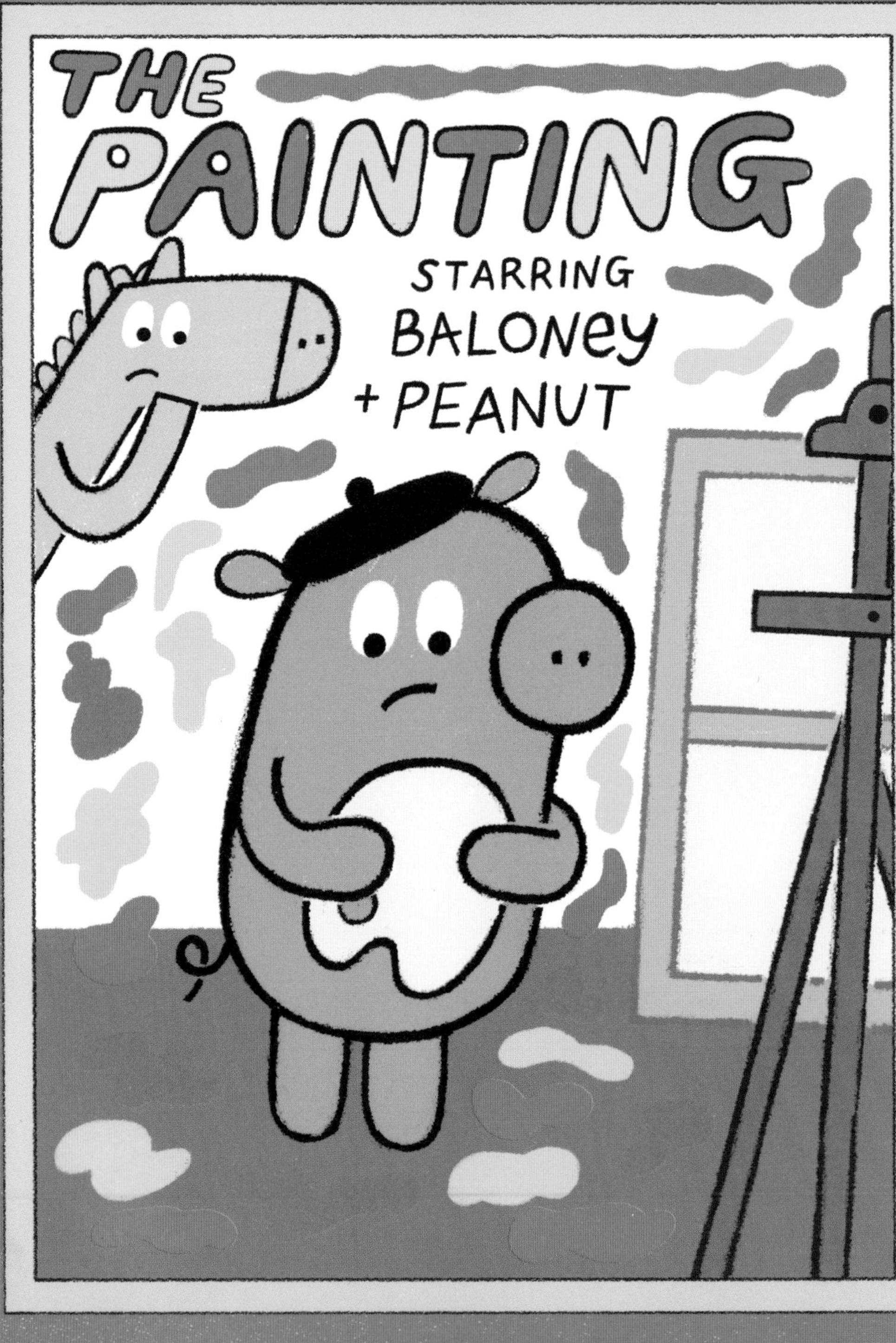

THE PAINTING
STARRING
BALONEY
+ PEANUT

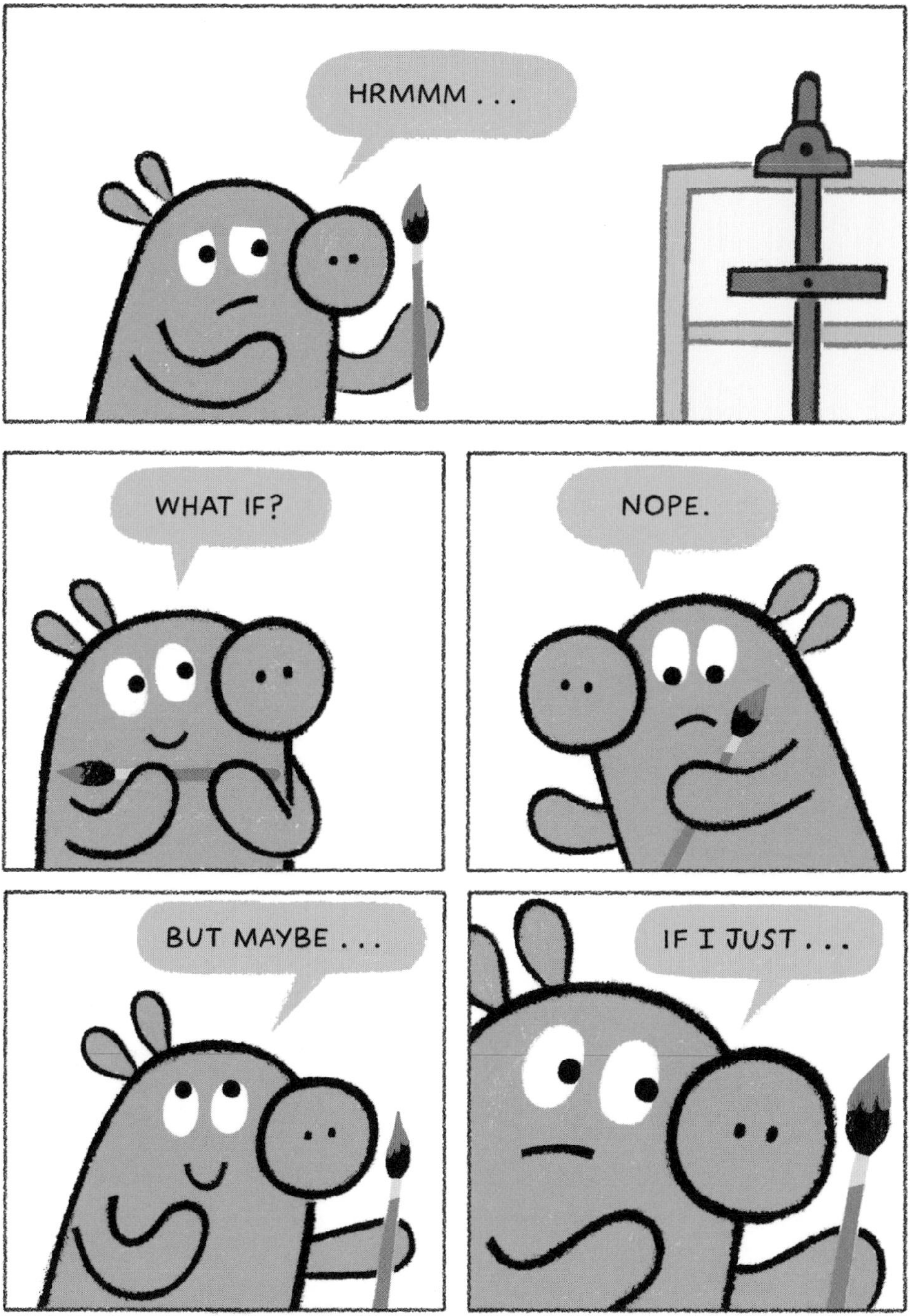
HRMMM . . .
WHAT IF?
NOPE.
BUT MAYBE . . .
IF I JUST . . .

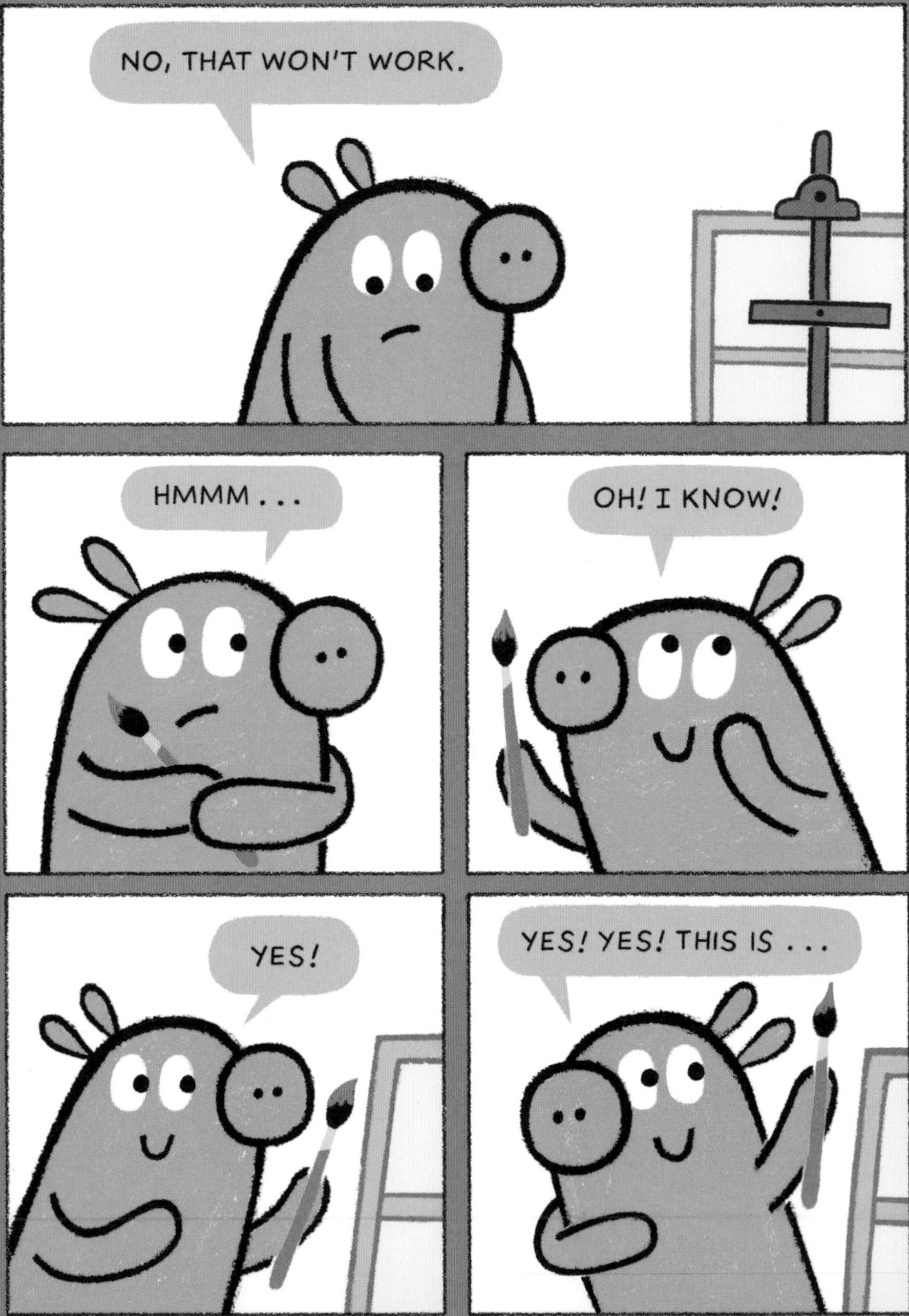
NO, THAT WON'T WORK.
HMMM . . .
OH! I KNOW!
YES!
YES! YES! THIS IS . . .

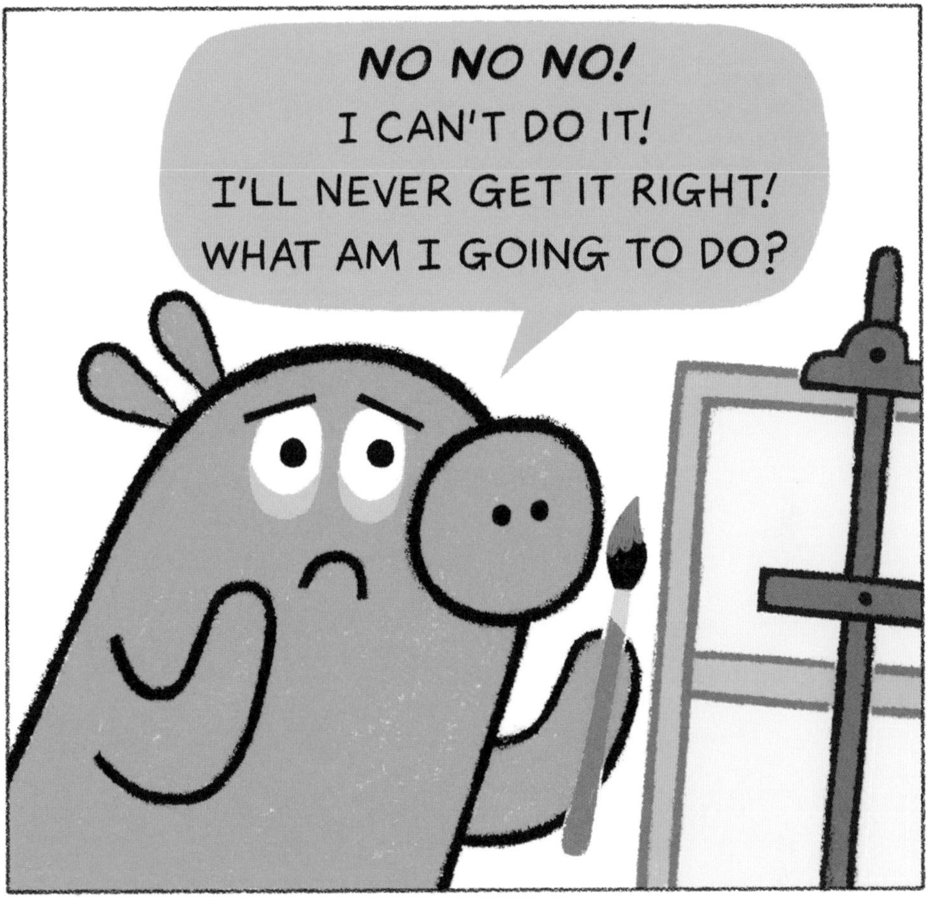
NO NO NO!
I CAN'T DO IT!
I'LL NEVER GET IT RIGHT!
WHAT AM I GOING TO DO?

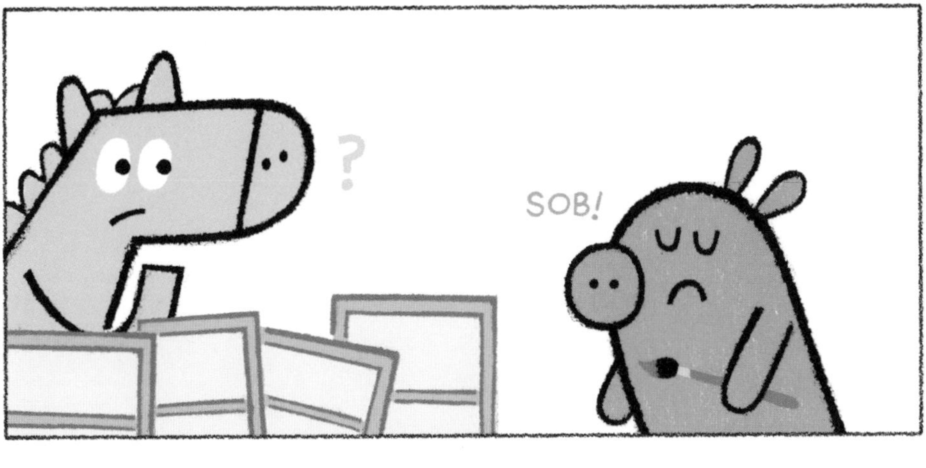
?
SOB!

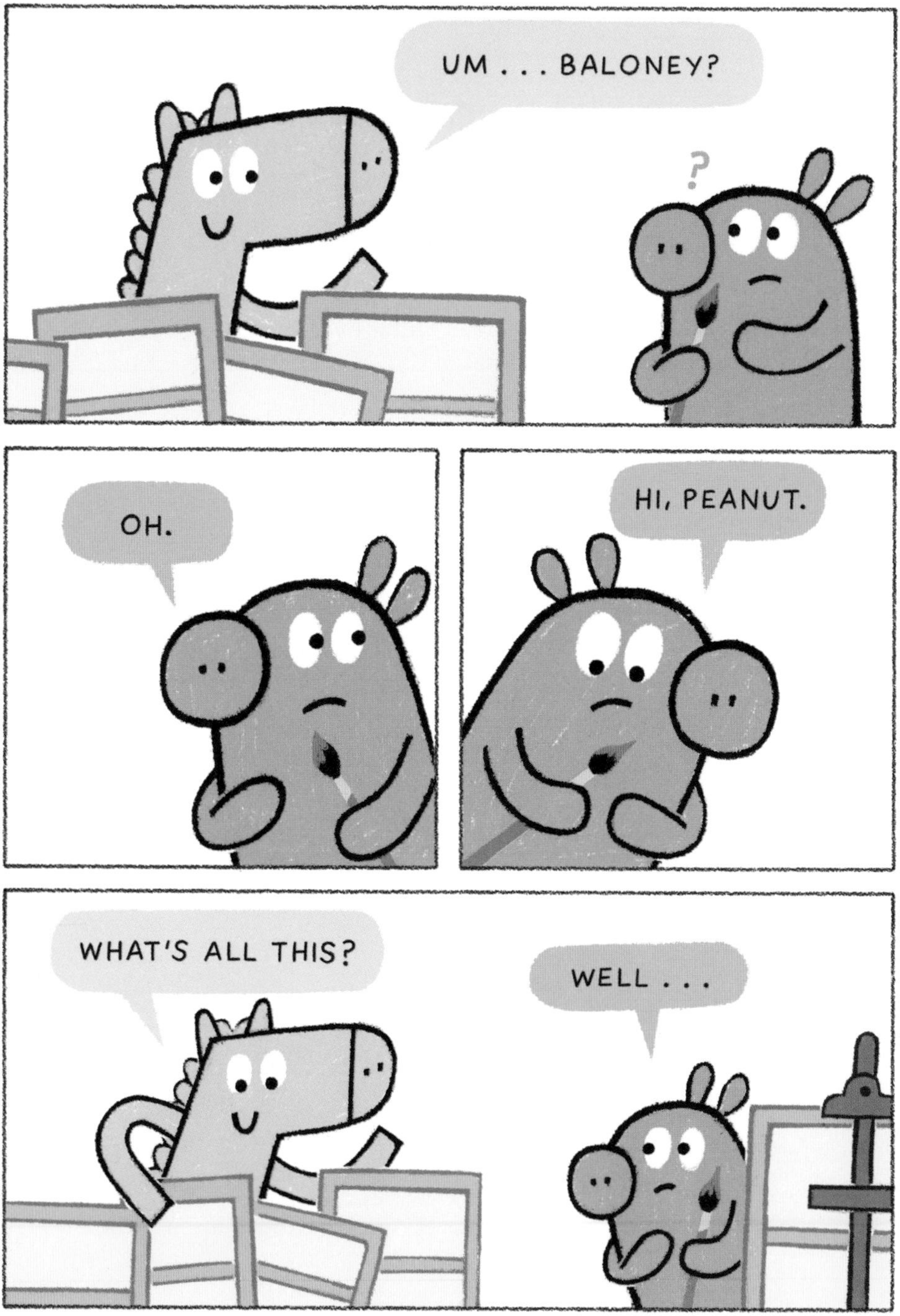
UM . . . BALONEY?
?
OH.
HI, PEANUT.
WHAT'S ALL THIS?
WELL . . .

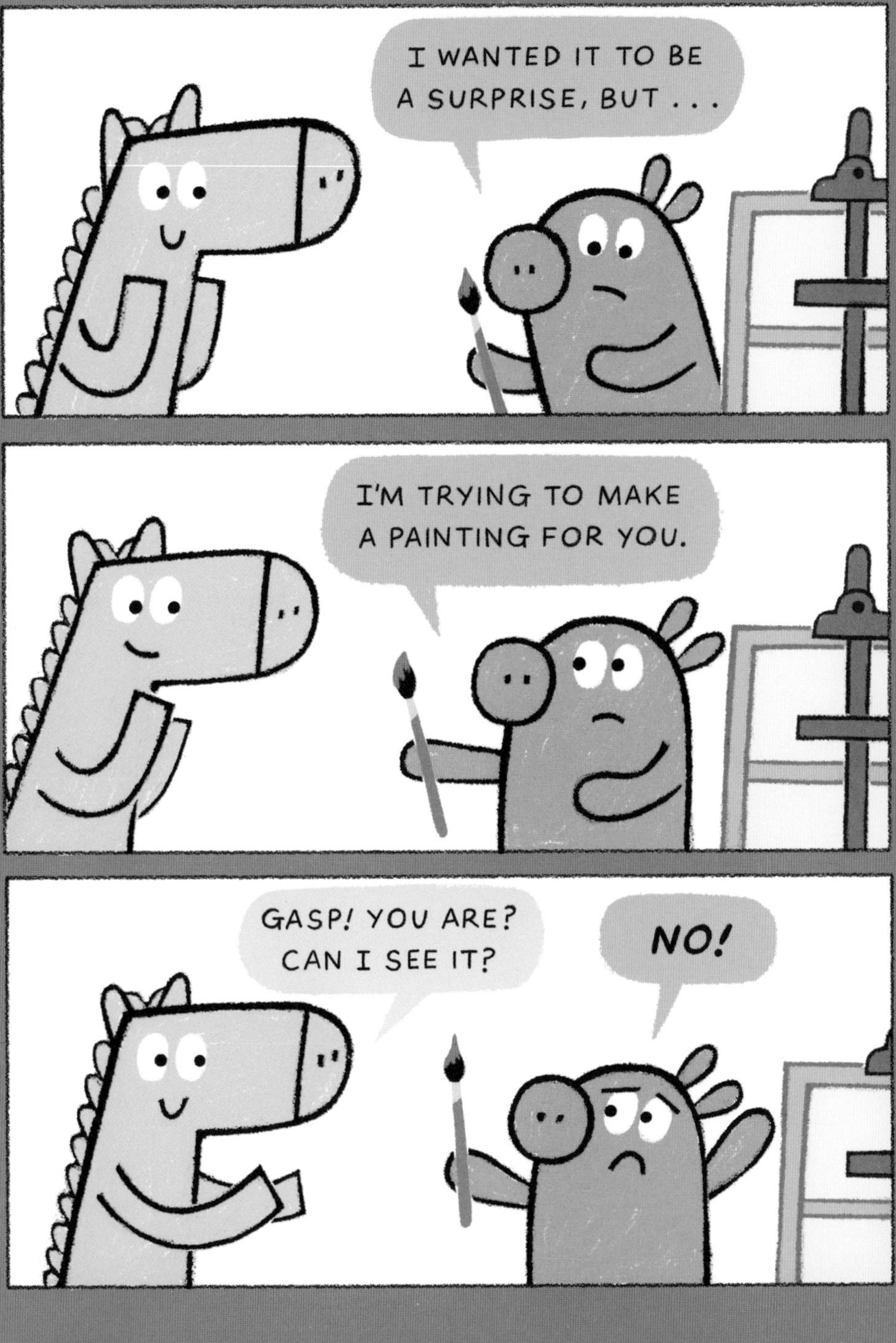
I WANTED IT TO BE A SURPRISE, BUT . . .
I'M TRYING TO MAKE A PAINTING FOR YOU.
GASP! YOU ARE? CAN I SEE IT?
NO!

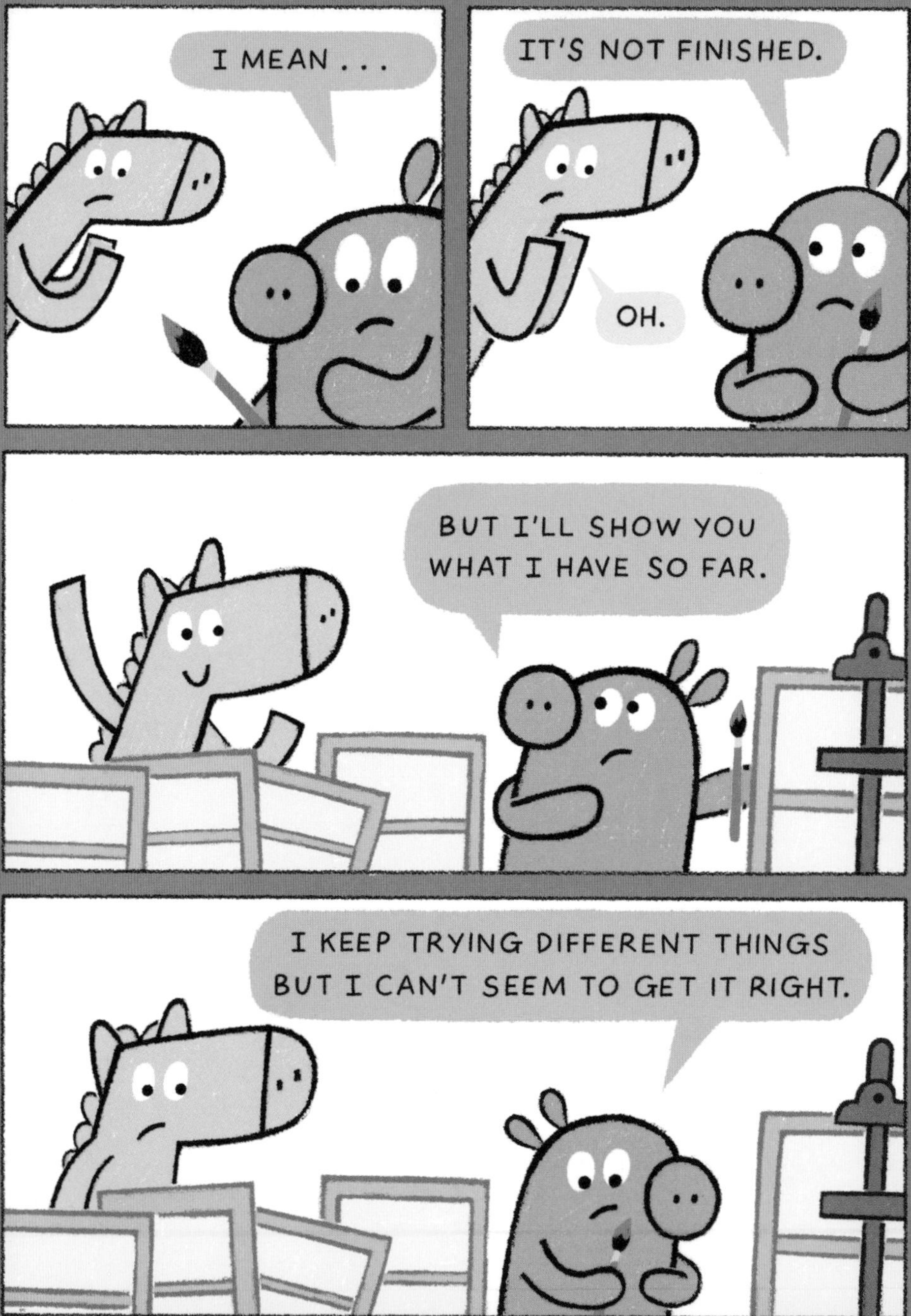
I MEAN . . .
IT'S NOT FINISHED.
OH.
BUT I'LL SHOW YOU WHAT I HAVE SO FAR.
I KEEP TRYING DIFFERENT THINGS BUT I CAN'T SEEM TO GET IT RIGHT.

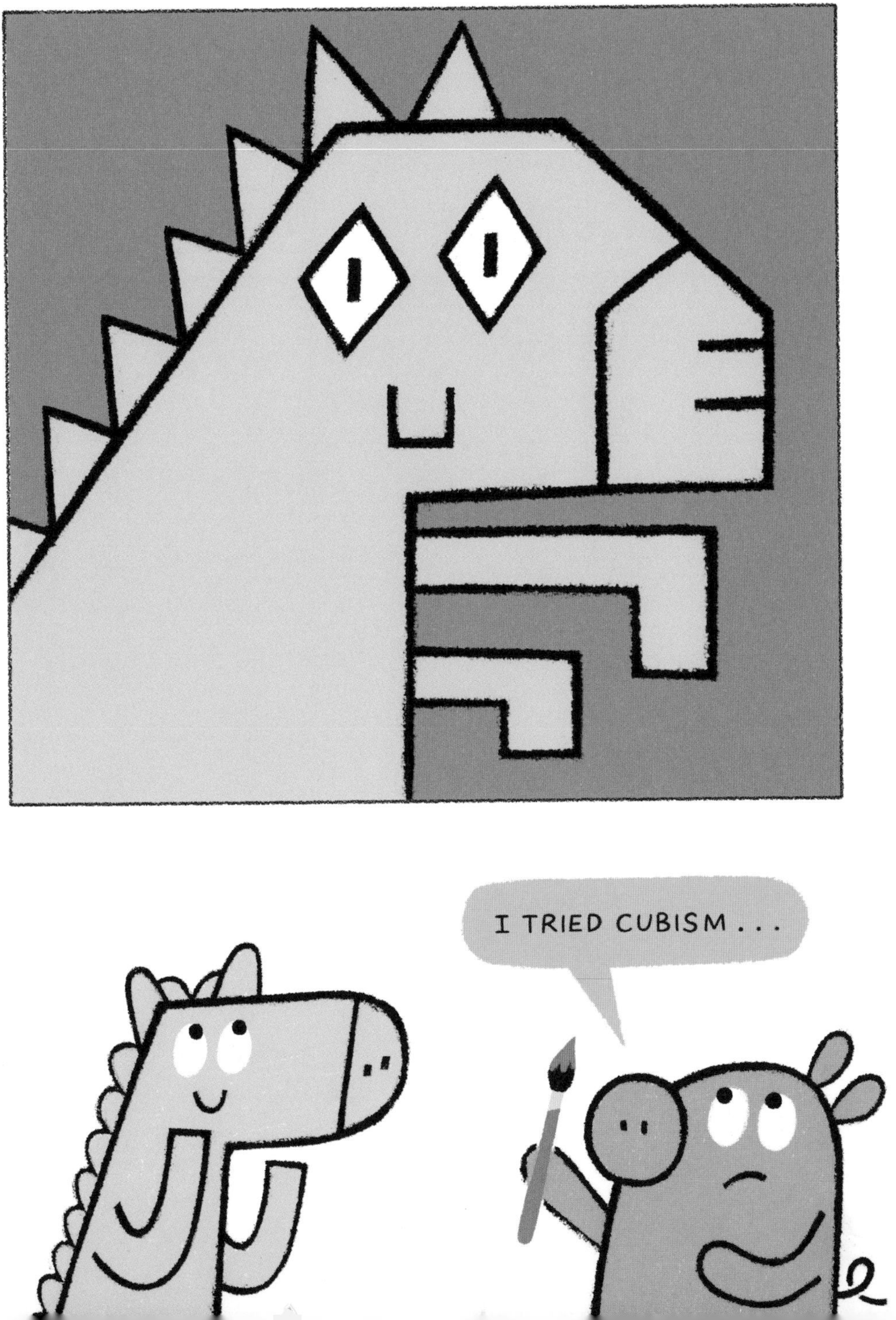
I TRIED CUBISM . . .

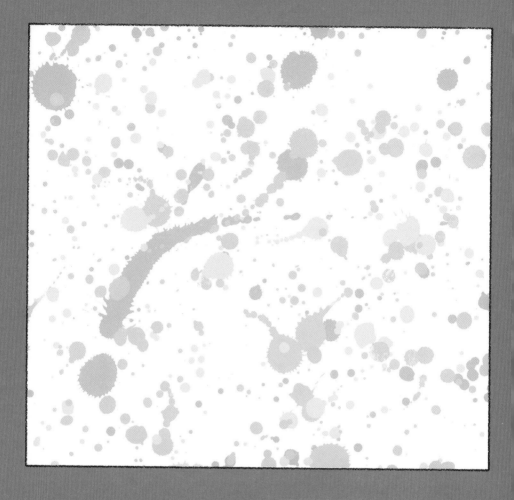

ABSTRACTION...

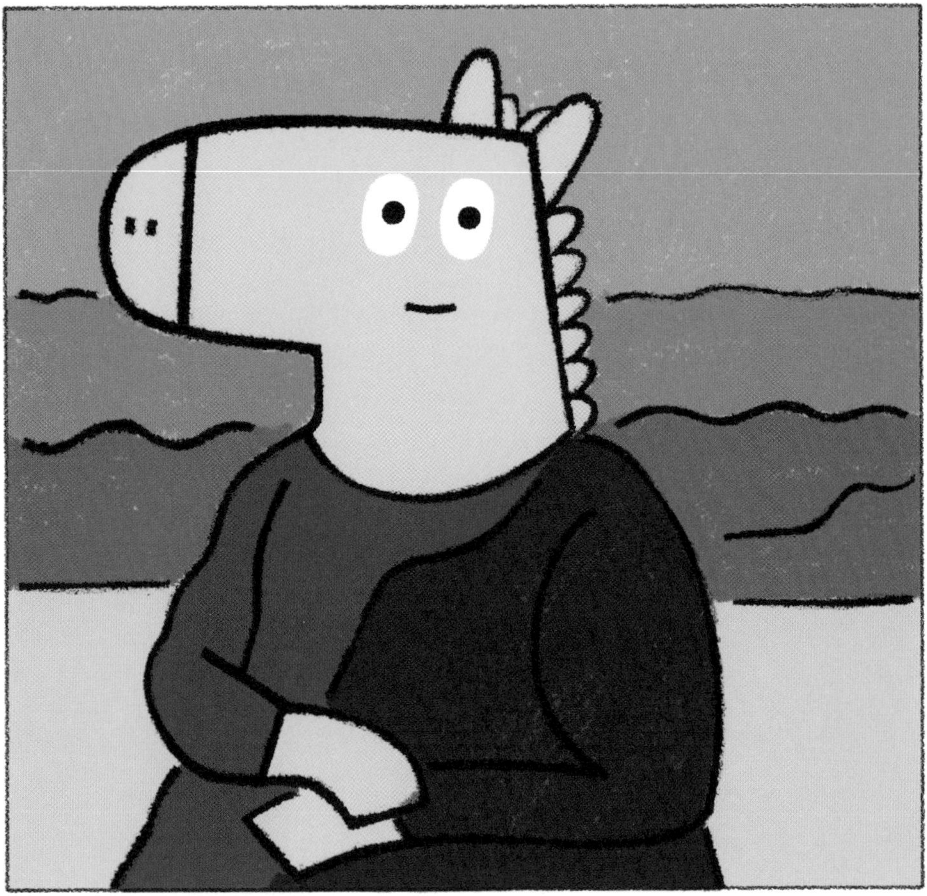

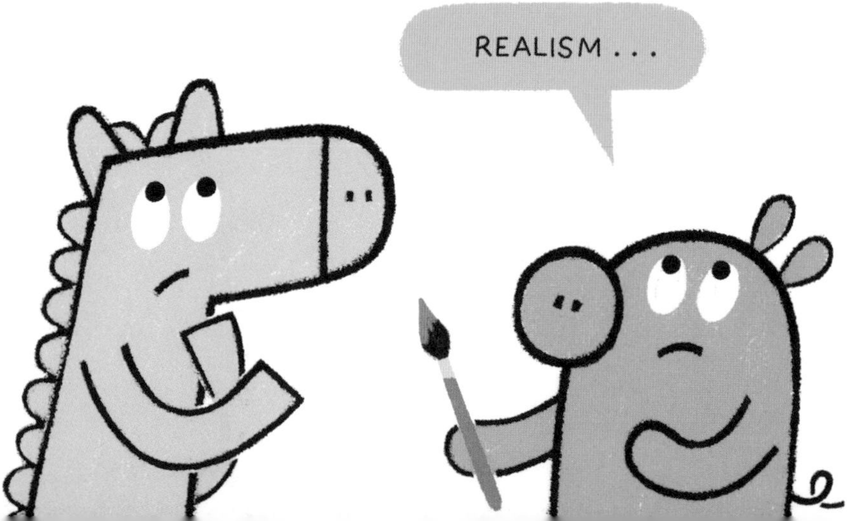
REALISM . . .

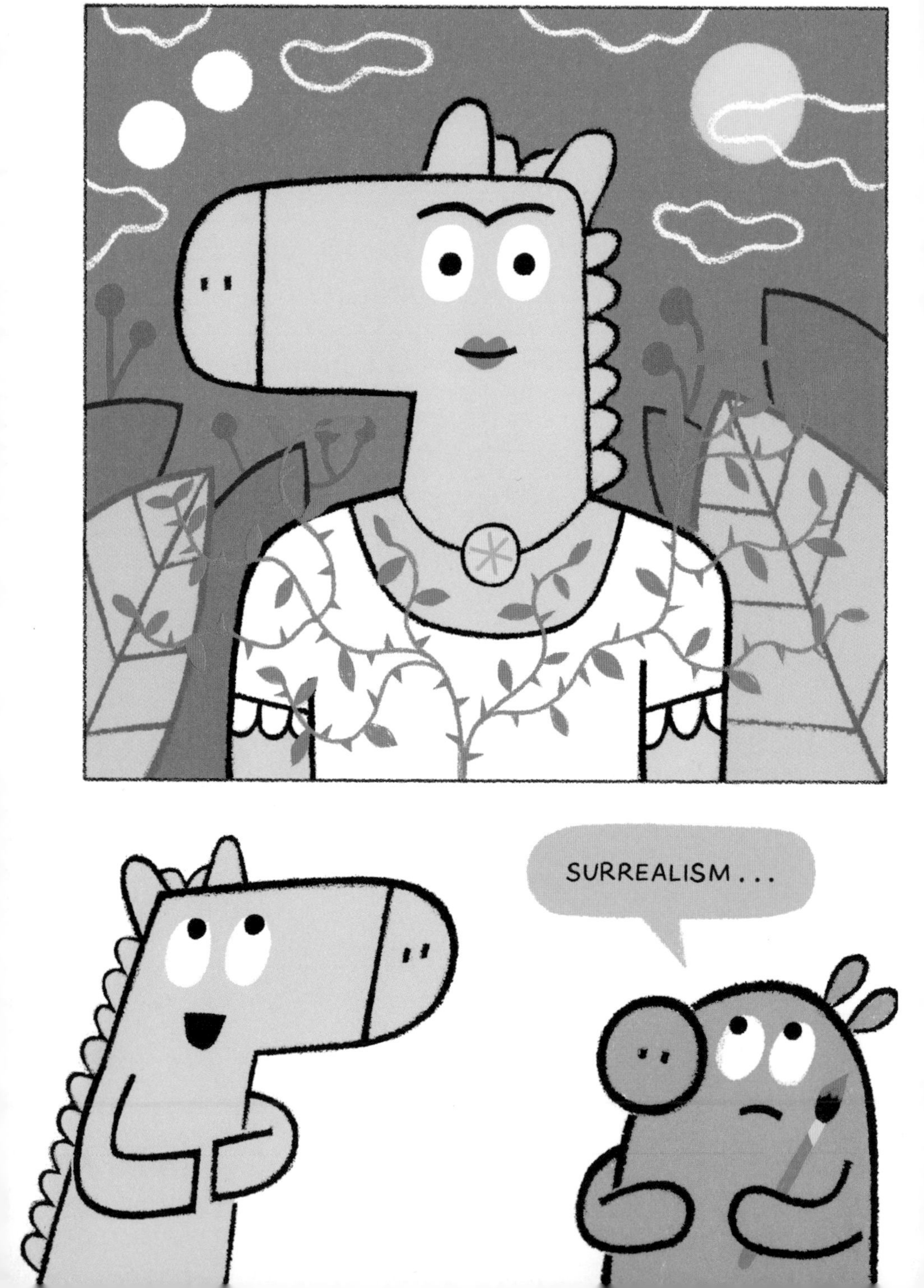
SURREALISM . . .

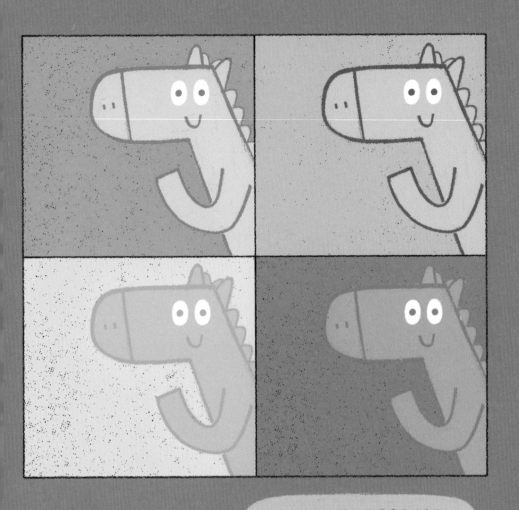

I EVEN TRIED POP ART.
BUT NOTHING SEEMS RIGHT.

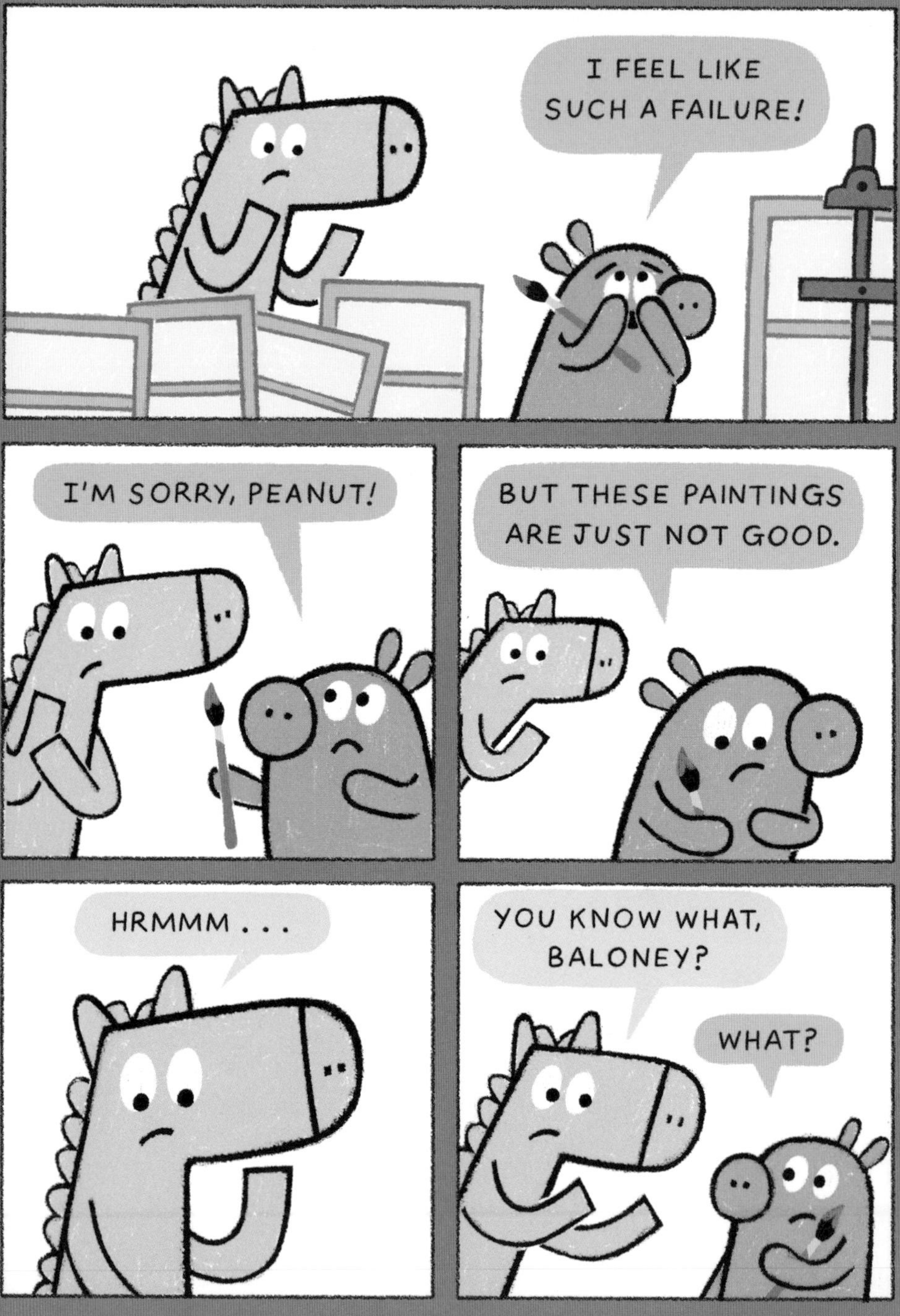
I FEEL LIKE SUCH A FAILURE!
I'M SORRY, PEANUT!
BUT THESE PAINTINGS ARE JUST NOT GOOD.
HRMMM . . .
YOU KNOW WHAT, BALONEY?
WHAT?

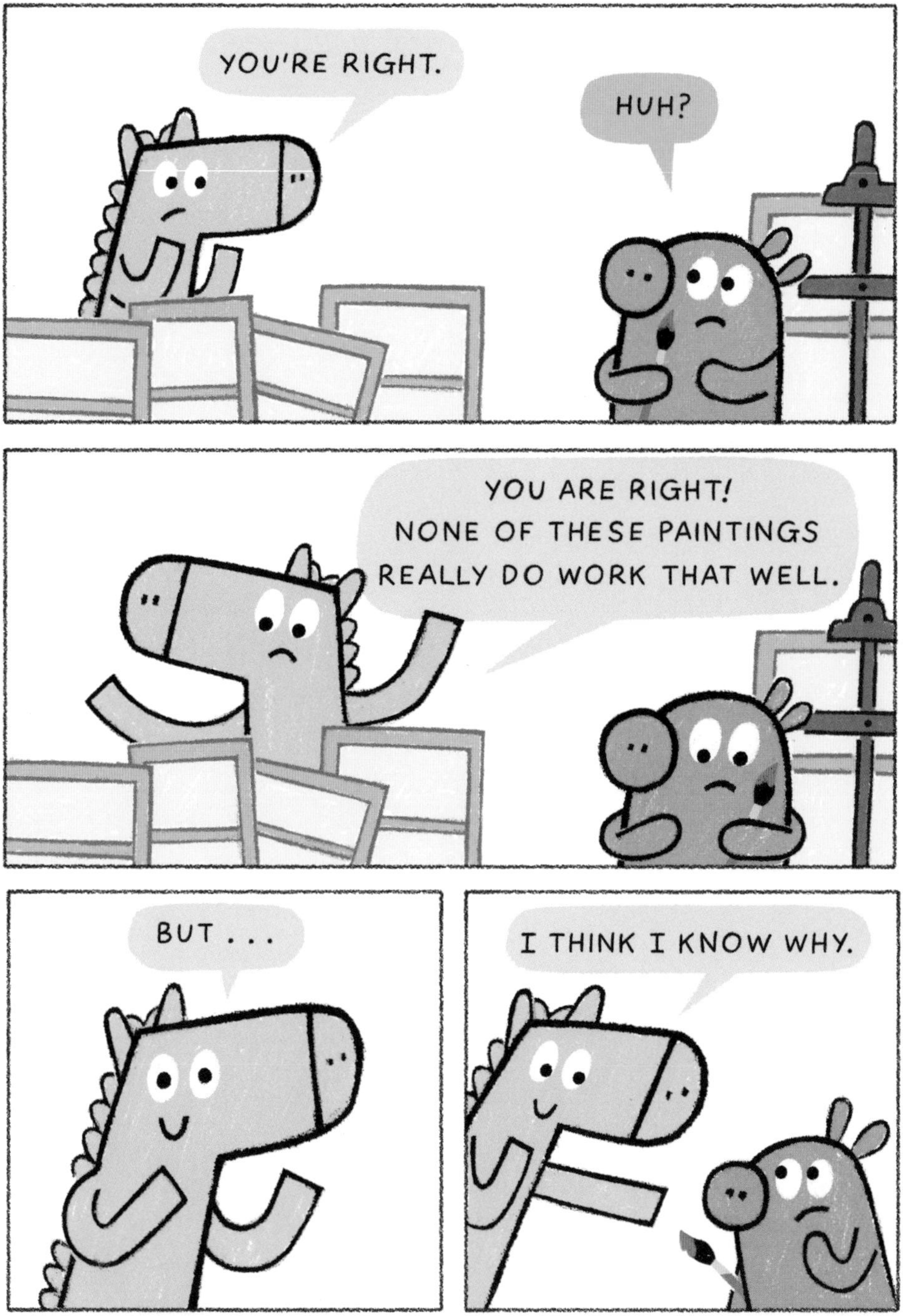
YOU'RE RIGHT.
HUH?
YOU ARE RIGHT! NONE OF THESE PAINTINGS REALLY DO WORK THAT WELL.
BUT . . .
I THINK I KNOW WHY.

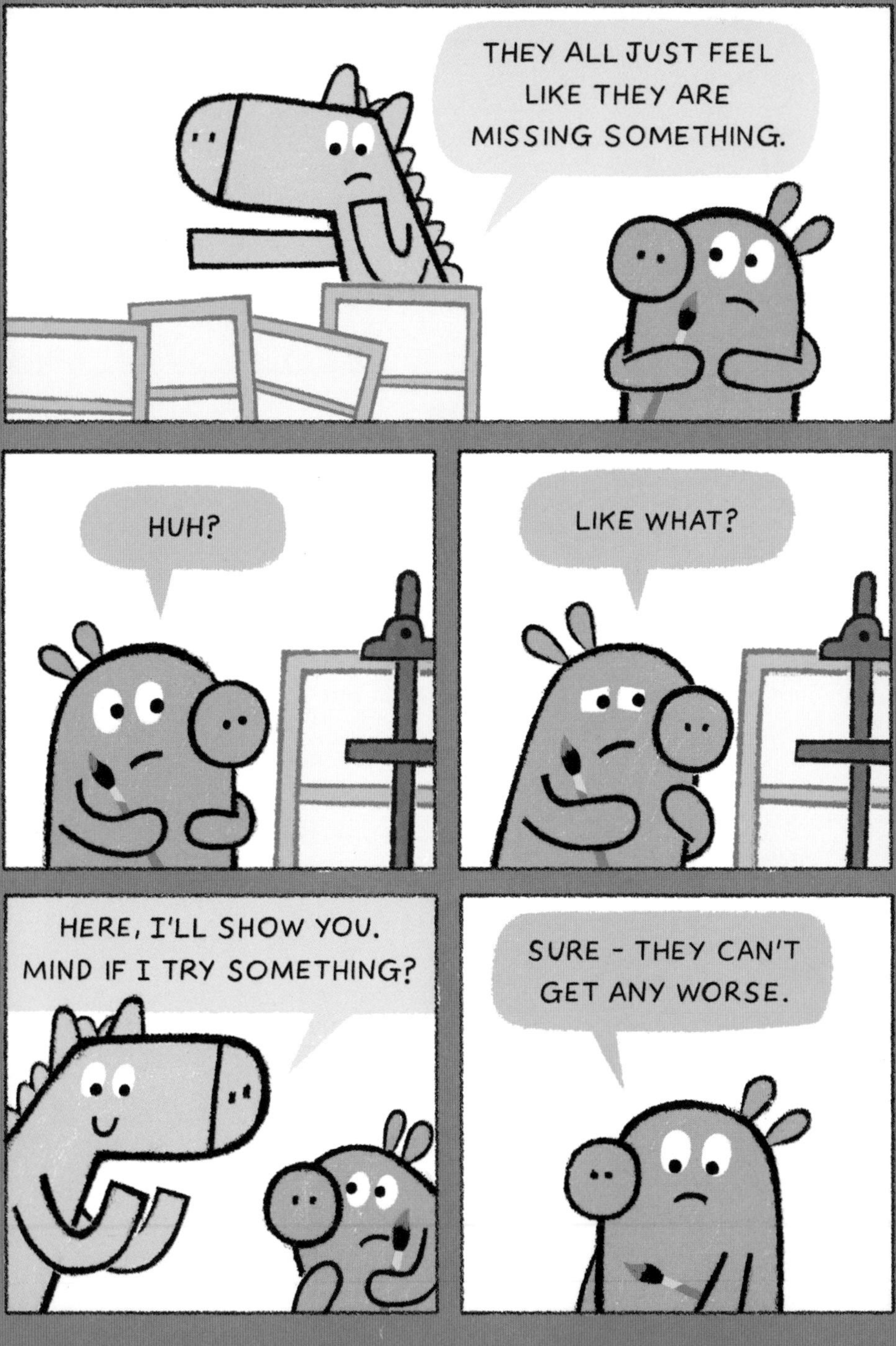
THEY ALL JUST FEEL LIKE THEY ARE MISSING SOMETHING.
HUH?
LIKE WHAT?
HERE, I'LL SHOW YOU. MIND IF I TRY SOMETHING?
SURE - THEY CAN'T GET ANY WORSE.

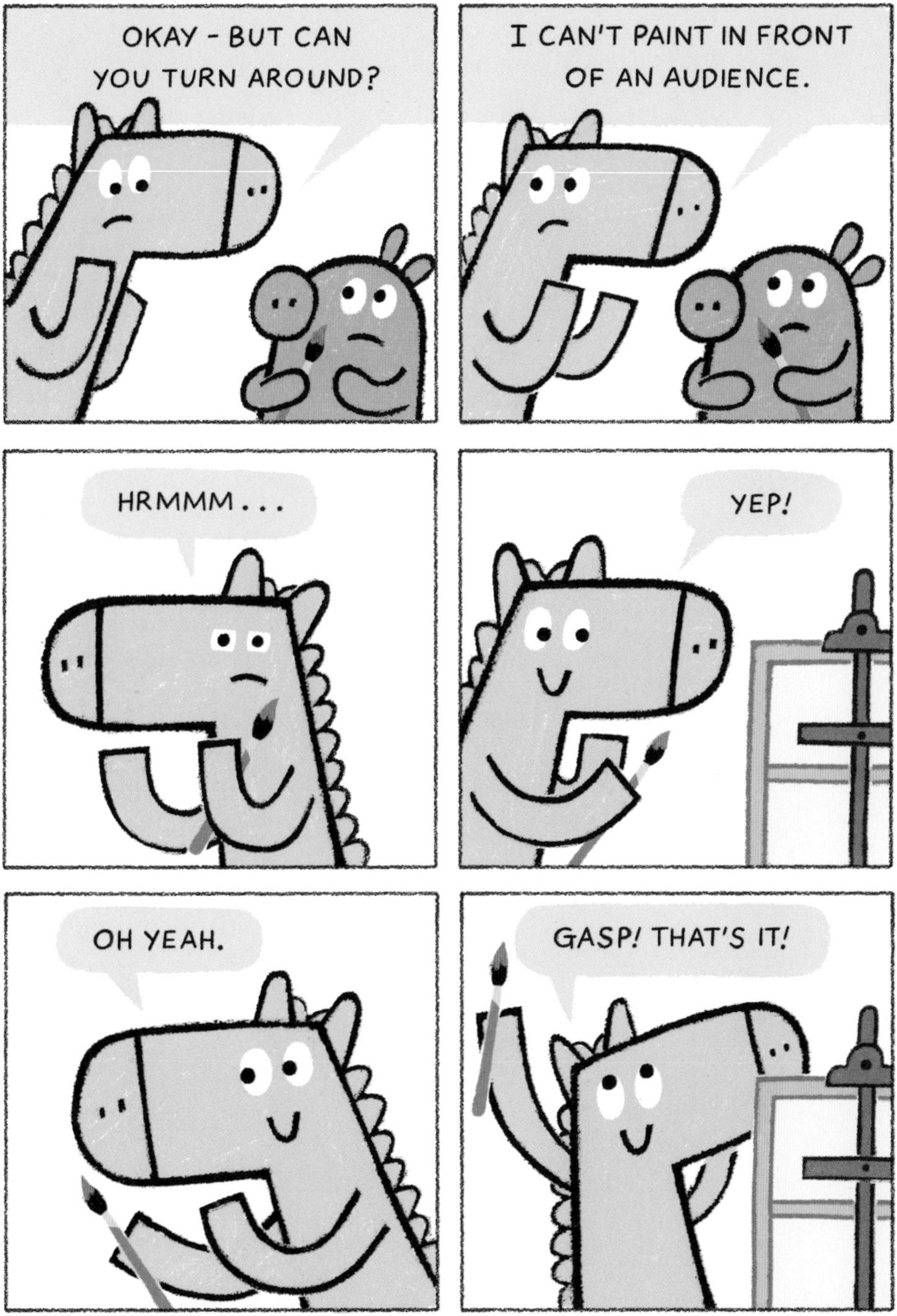
OKAY - BUT CAN YOU TURN AROUND?
I CAN'T PAINT IN FRONT OF AN AUDIENCE.
HRMMM...
YEP!
OH YEAH.
GASP! THAT'S IT!

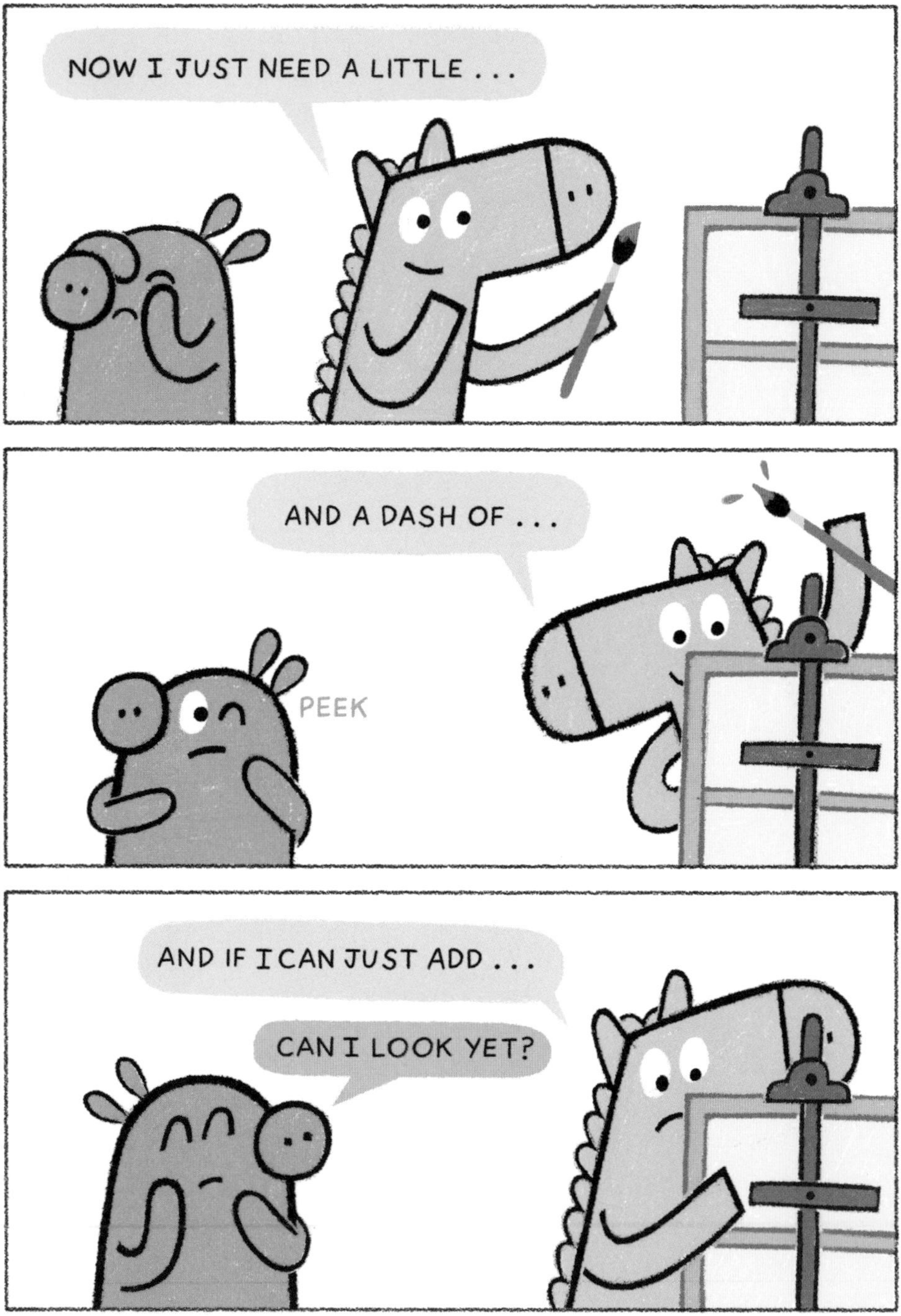
NOW I JUST NEED A LITTLE . . .
AND A DASH OF . . .
PEEK
AND IF I CAN JUST ADD . . .
CAN I LOOK YET?

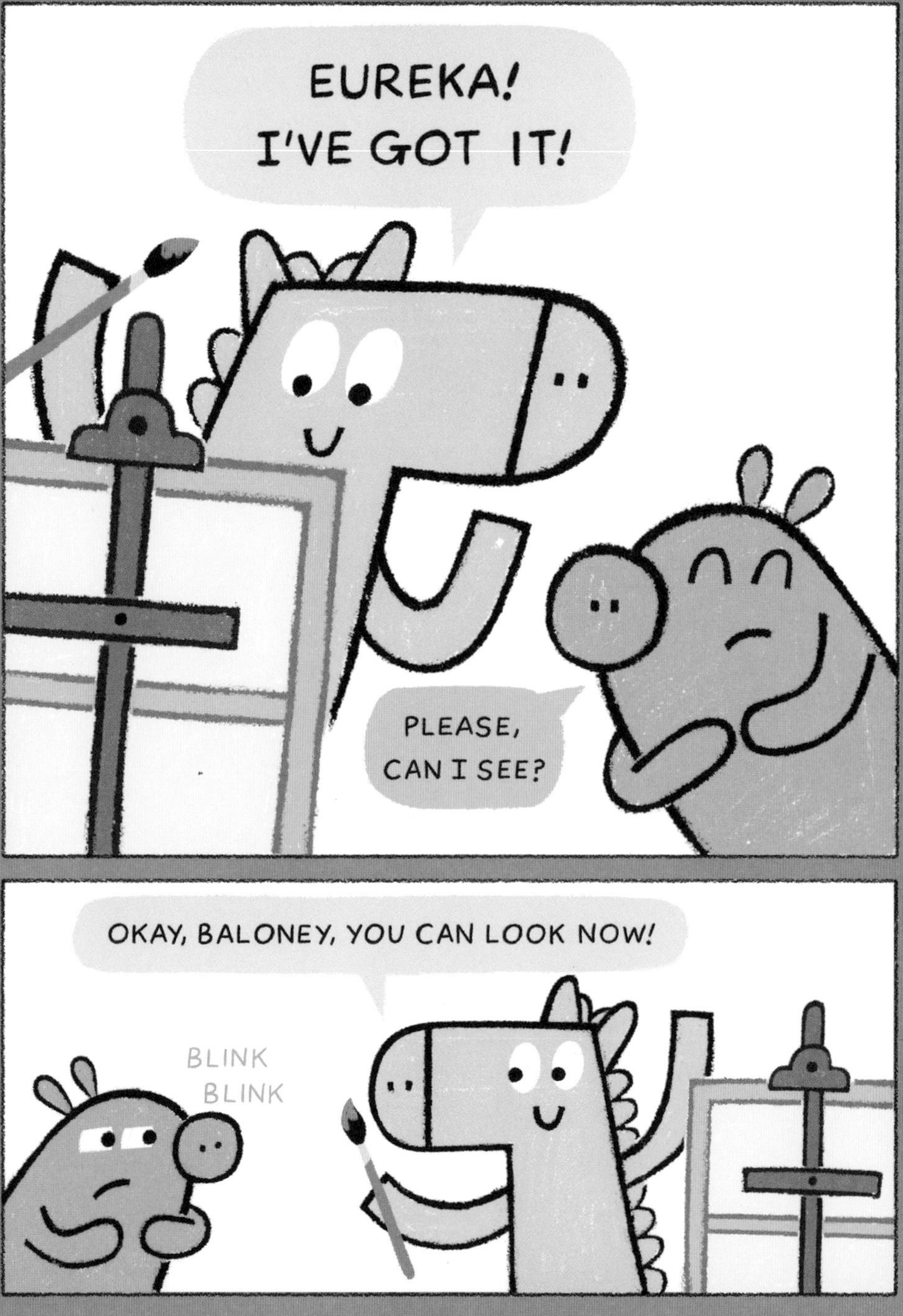
EUREKA! I'VE GOT IT!
PLEASE, CAN I SEE?
OKAY, BALONEY, YOU CAN LOOK NOW!
BLINK BLINK

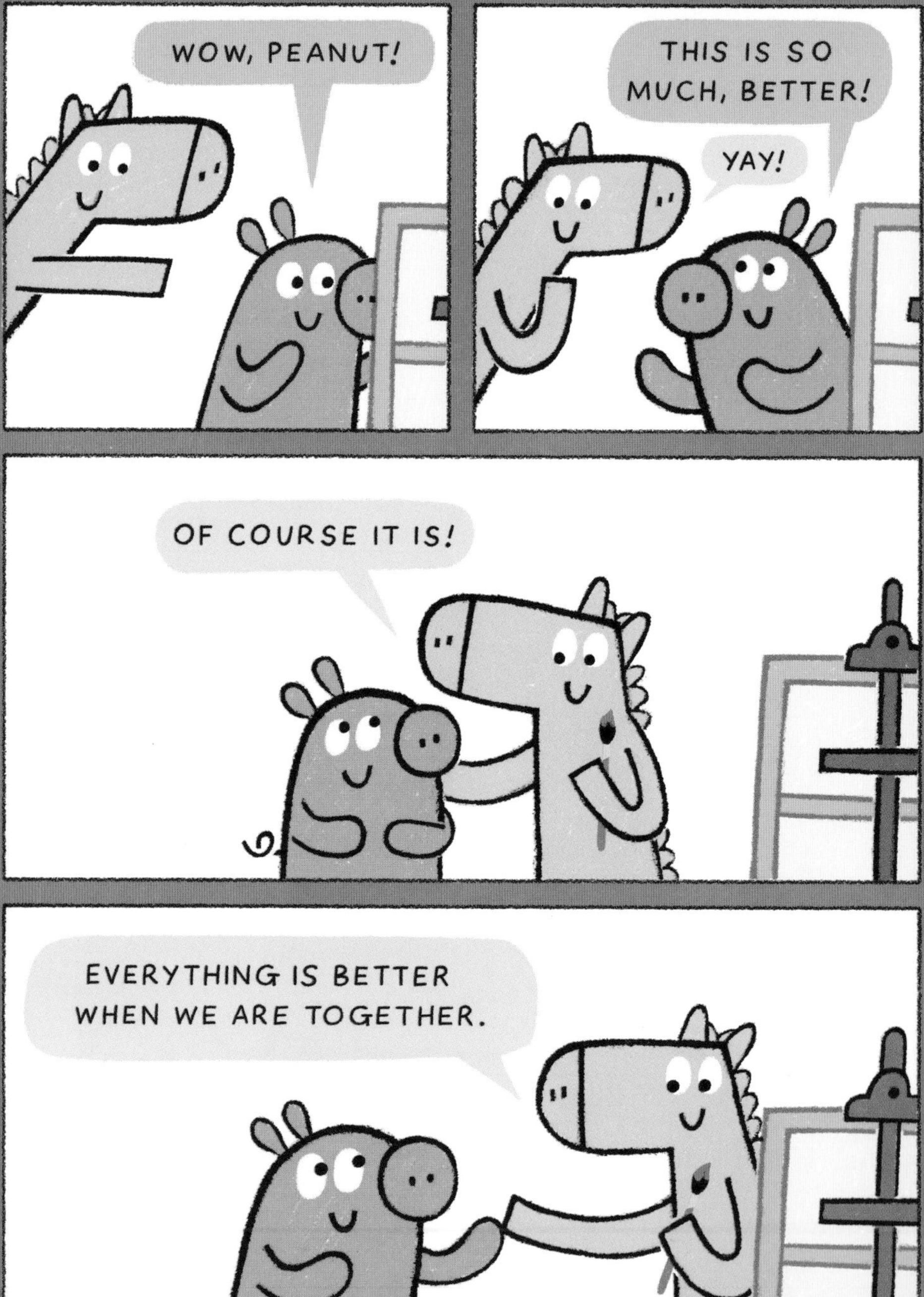
WOW, PEANUT!
THIS IS SO MUCH, BETTER!
YAY!
OF COURSE IT IS!
EVERYTHING IS BETTER WHEN WE ARE TOGETHER.

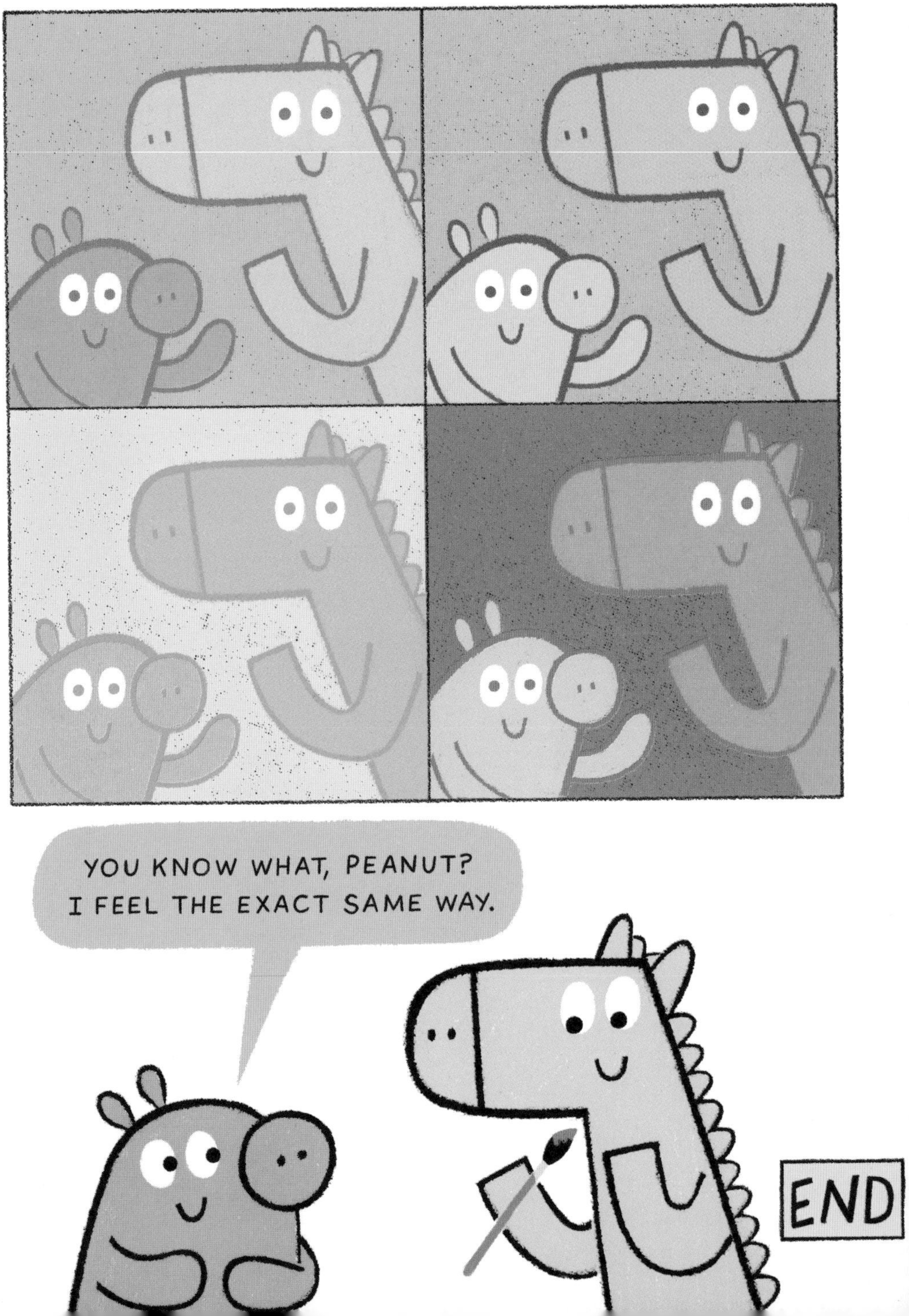
YOU KNOW WHAT, PEANUT?
I FEEL THE EXACT SAME WAY.
END

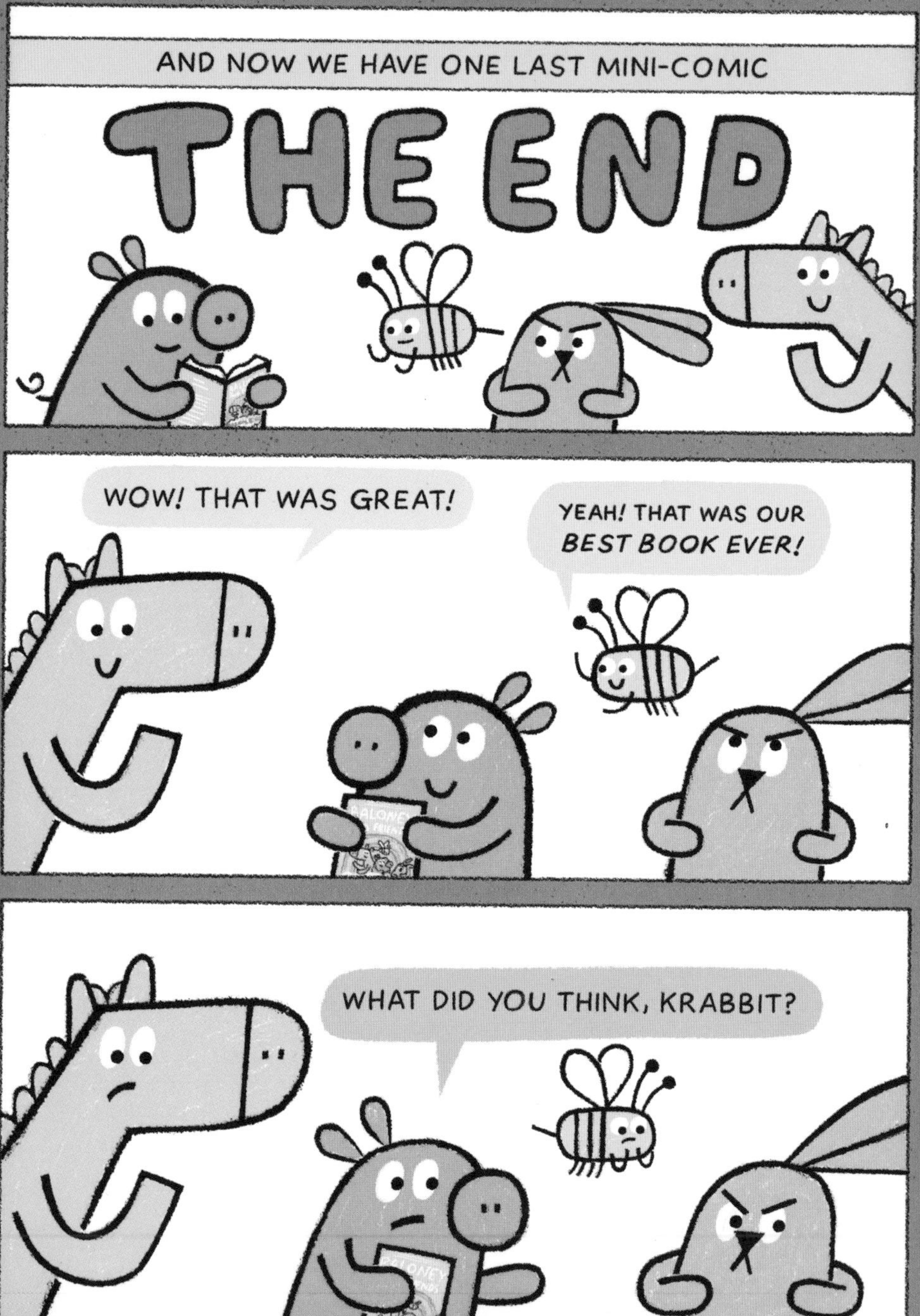
AND NOW WE HAVE ONE LAST MINI-COMIC
THE END
WOW! THAT WAS GREAT!
YEAH! THAT WAS OUR *BEST BOOK EVER!*
WHAT DID YOU THINK, KRABBIT?

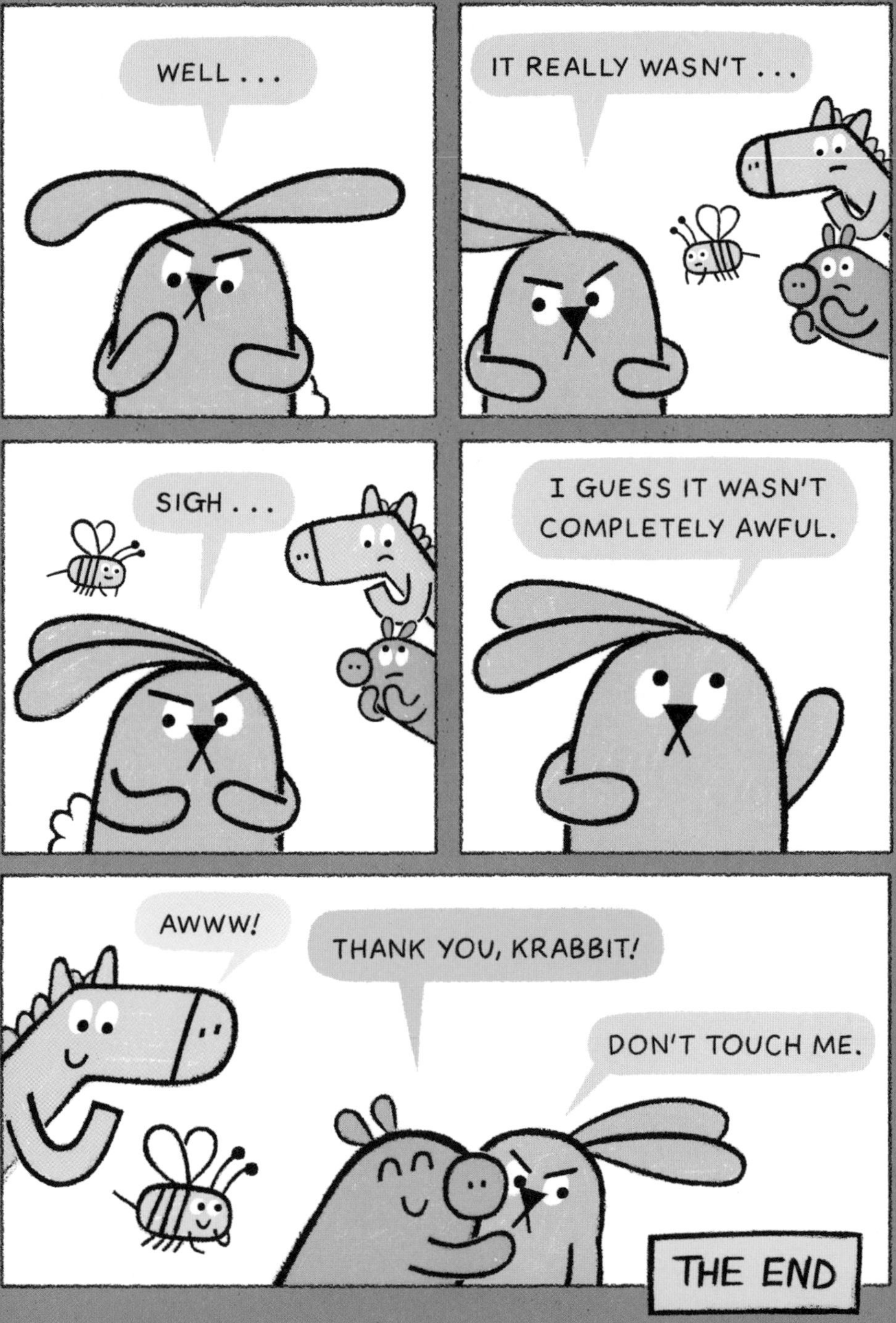
WELL . . .
IT REALLY WASN'T . . .
SIGH . . .
I GUESS IT WASN'T COMPLETELY AWFUL.
AWWW!
THANK YOU, KRABBIT!
DON'T TOUCH ME.
THE END

HOW TO MAKE A MINI-BOOK

SUPPLIES YOU WILL NEED:
- PAPER
- SCISSORS
- PENCIL
- A SENSE OF HUMOR

SHOULD WE TRY IT?

LET'S DO IT!

INSTRUCTIONS

FOLLOW THESE SEVEN STEPS TO MAKE YOUR OWN BOOK!

PRO TIP: READ EACH STEP BEFORE FOLDING OR CUTTING YOUR PAPER!

STEP ONE

FOLD THE SHEET OF PAPER IN HALF LONGWAYS (HOT DOG FOLD).

STEP TWO

OPEN THE PAPER BACK UP AND THEN FOLD IT IN HALF IN THE OTHER DIRECTION (HAMBURGER FOLD).

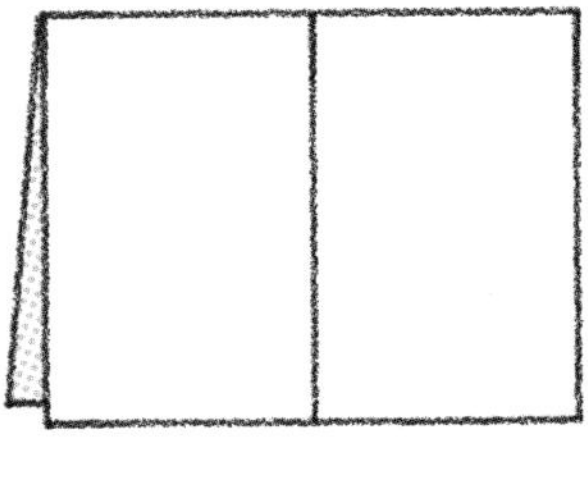

STEP THREE

FOLD EACH HALF OF YOUR "HAMBURGER" IN TO MEET THE CENTERFOLD.

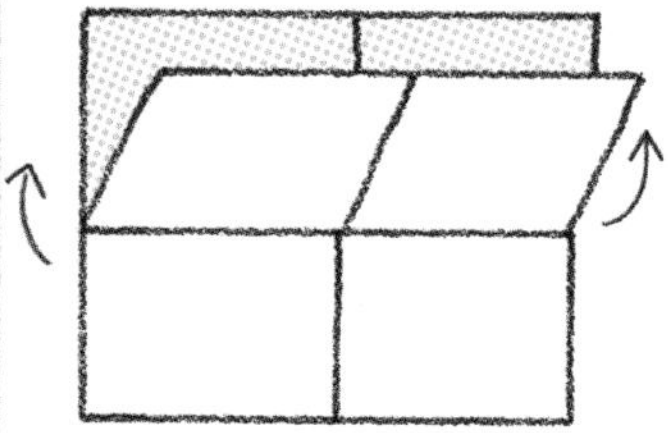

NEXT, UNFOLD YOUR PAPER. YOUR SHEET SHOULD NOW HAVE EIGHT PANELS.

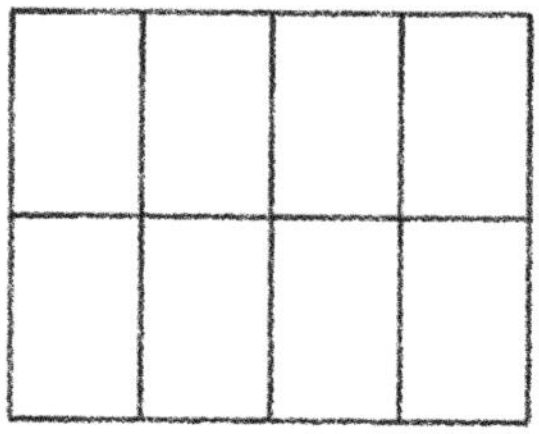

STEP FOUR

REFOLD THE PAPER LIKE A HAMBURGER. CAREFULLY CUT ALONG THE CENTERFOLD, MAKING SURE TO ONLY CUT THROUGH THE MIDDLE TWO PANELS.

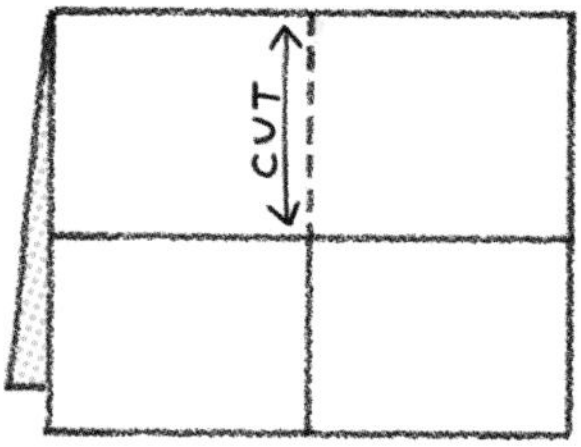
CUT

STEP FIVE

REFOLD THE PAPER LIKE A HOT DOG, THEN PUSH THE ENDS TOWARD THE CENTER, AND CLOSE THE BOOK.

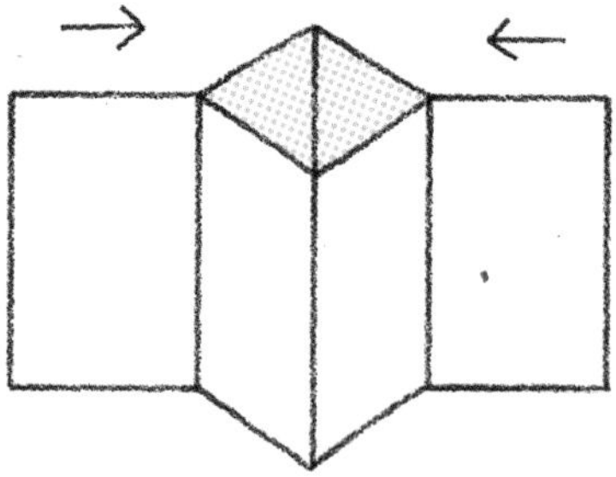

FLATTEN YOUR BOOK INTO
A STACK OF NEAT PAGES WITH
A FRONT AND BACK COVER.

CREASE THE FOLD ONE MORE
TIME TO MAKE THE BOOK EXTRA
EASY TO OPEN AND CLOSE.

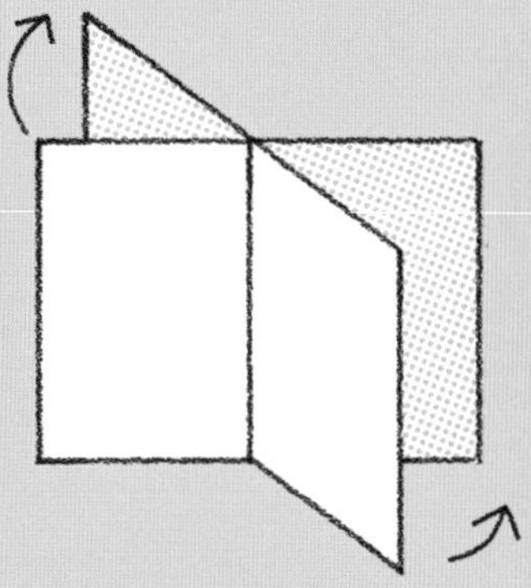

S
T
E
P

S
E
V
E
N

FILL YOUR BOOK WITH
DRAWINGS, COMICS, POETRY,
OR ANYTHING YOU LIKE!

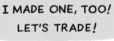

YOU
MADE
A
BOOK!

FINALLY!
MY OWN BOOK.

I MADE ONE, TOO!
LET'S TRADE!

THINGS
I LIKE
ABOUT
MYSELF
BY
BIZZ

RABBIT

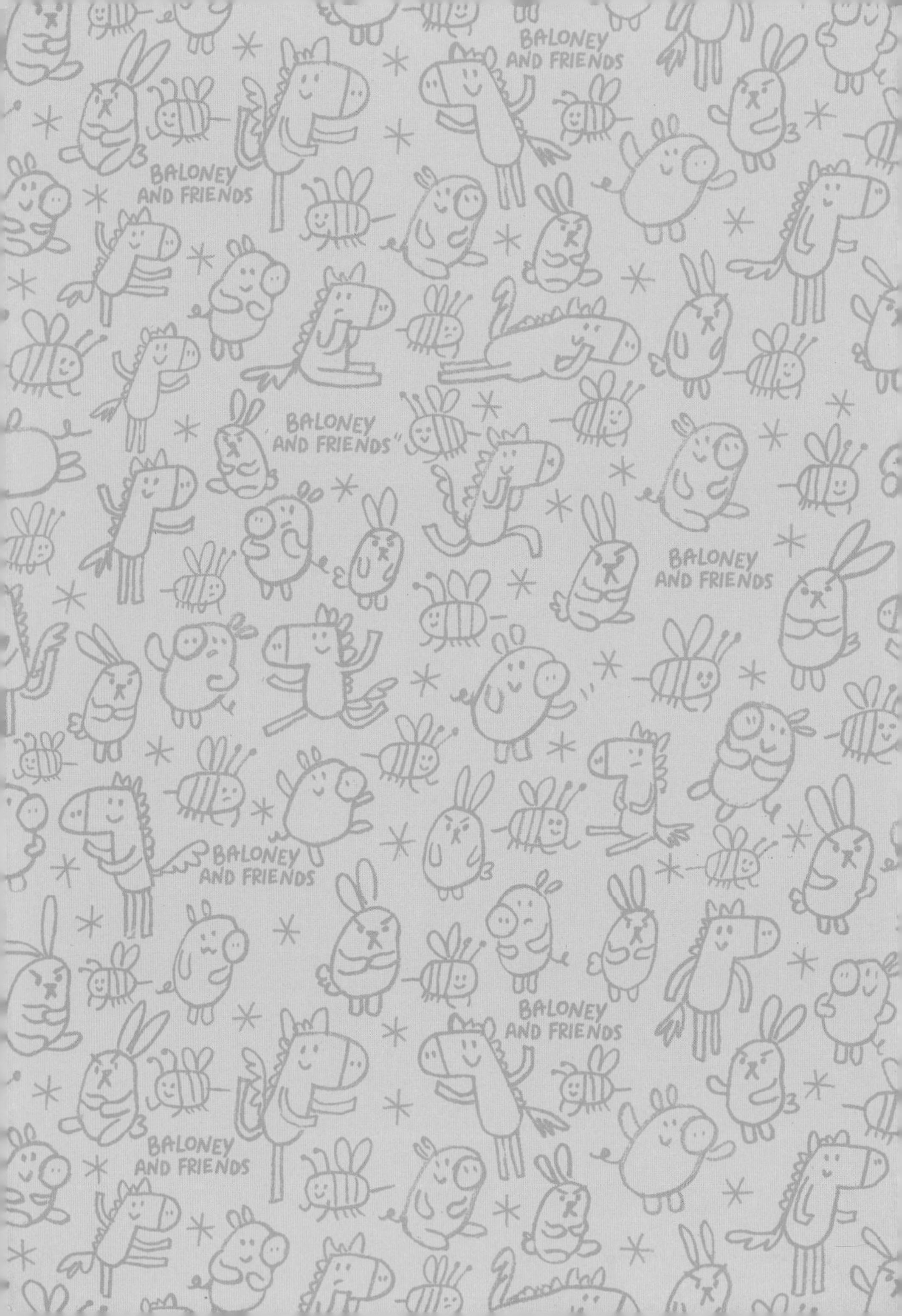
BALONEY
AND FRIENDS